Annabelle yearns for romance. She longs to be like the heroines whose exploits she follows in her beloved Fanny Sparrow novels. When her aunt and uncle invite her to go to Bath for the season, she feels as if her every dream is about to come true.

But reality and fantasy don't always see eye-to-eye, and even supposed friends can be hiding ugly truths. A chance encounter with a handsome man as she's attempting to escape a horrible miscreant sets Annabelle's heart to thumping and her imagination to running rampant.

Her uncle has just inherited Godshollow, a gothic castle hidden in the heart of the Gloucestershire countryside. Is Annabelle's long-awaited adventure about to begin? And will she survive it?

Godshollow
Copyright © 2019 Catherine Price
ISBN: 978-1-4874-2703-0
Cover art by Martine Jardin

Published by eXtasy Books Inc or
Devine Destinies, an imprint of eXtasy Books Inc

Look for us online at:
www.eXtasybooks.com or www.devinedestinies.com

GODSHOLLOW

BY

CATHERINE PRICE

Merry Christmas!

With love,

 CP xx

DEDICATION

*Hi everyone *waves**

For Anne. No, not in that way. Thank you for encouraging me and making me think I was a good writer.

For David. Yes, in that way. No Fabio will ever compare to you, sweetie.

CHAPTER ONE

"Is that them?" At a sound from outside, Annabelle charged towards the window and pressed her face against the glass.

"No, dear. That's the chickens. Like it was Farmer Johnson before that, and a tree before that. They'll be here soon," her father assured her. "They are by no means late. Try to relax and wait for them. You could read one of your books."

Annabelle glanced at the book that lay open on the table beside her. It was the latest offering from her favourite author, Fanny Sparrow, but she hadn't gotten very far. She hadn't been able to sit down long enough to read more than a few lines. A bookmark was settled quite comfortably between the pages, holding the place that hadn't been changed for at least half an hour.

"I wish they would hurry," she huffed petulantly.

"I'm sure they're going as fast as they can, my dear," her father replied calmly.

Annabelle cast a sheepish glance at her trunks piled out in the hallway. "Perhaps I'll check my luggage again."

"Annabelle. Sit down," her father commanded. "My dear, I think you have packed everything quite meticulously. You have nearly the whole house in there, save for the cat. It will only be for a few weeks."

Annabelle slowly dropped back into her seat and faced her father.

"I know," she replied, worrying the sleeve of her dress. "But I feel sure I've forgotten something, and I know that I

1

won't think of it until I am in *dire* need of it. By then it will be useless to remember it at all." She sighed dramatically. "What if I meet a dashing young officer only to find that I've left my handkerchief behind? How will he be able to introduce himself if I have no token to offer him?"

From her position in the doorway, Annabelle's mother gave her a worried look. "Annabelle, darling, I know this trip is very exciting for you, but are you sure you aren't overthinking this? Real life isn't like novels, even if we wish it to be so."

Annabelle knew life wasn't like the novels she loved so much. But a girl could dream, couldn't she? True, she did have very high hopes for this trip. Deep down she felt this would be the defining experience of her eighteen years of life.

Which was why she was so impatient for her aunt and uncle to arrive.

"Just one last check?" she bartered. Her parents relented and allowed her to peruse the contents of her luggage once more.

"At least it will give her something to do," Annabelle heard her father comment to his wife.

She was in the middle of refolding her extra-extra pair of stockings when her mother came up behind her.

"I think I hear someone at the door."

Mrs Knight had hardly finished her sentence before Annabelle was on her feet and rushing away. Seconds later she ran back.

"They're here, they're here!"

She promptly returned to her guests—who in the meantime had been admitted—bombarding them with questions.

"When will we be leaving? How long will it take to get to Bath? Yes, yes, it's good to see you, too, but what will we do once we're there? How many places will we visit on the first day?"

Her uncle chuckled kindly. "All in good time," was all he

would say.

Mrs Knight soon joined her daughter to welcome the Daniels and led them into the parlour. "Would you care for some breakfast, Colin?" She signalled for the maid.

The visitor shook his head. "We must be going soon. We would prefer to get to Bath today, if at all possible."

Annabelle stifled a giggle when, behind him, his wife made a pitiable face of disappointment over the loss of breakfast.

"What's that?" Annabelle asked as Mr Daniels laid a piece of paper on the table. She tilted her head to examine the writing.

Mr Daniels laughed. "It's a map. Dear me, what *are* you young people learning about these days?"

"I know it's a map," Annabelle pointed out with a smile. Her uncle loved to tease her. "What is it a map *of*?"

"Ah . . ." Her uncle tapped the side of his nose conspiratorially. "This is the map for the new property that's come into my possession."

Annabelle twisted her neck farther to read the upside-down writing. "Godshollow?" she asked with much excitement.

"Yes," Mr Daniels replied. "It's a large Gothic house in Gloucestershire. The estate was originally owned by an old army acquaintance of mine. Seems he's left it to me in his will. I have no idea why, but I'm never one to look a gift horse in the mouth. We were intending to visit the property for a month or so after we brought you home from Bath. That's why I have all the paperwork with me."

Annabelle had been captured by the word gothic, but her face dropped as she did, falling to her knees. "Please say I can come with you?" she begged. "Please! It sounds the most wonderful thing in the world. And I've never seen a real Gothic home before. Please, Uncle, please?"

Mr Daniels turned to his wife, then to his sister and

brother-in-law. "I can't see why not," he said hesitantly. "But it's your parents' decision. That would mean an extra few weeks away. Does that sound agreeable, Jack?"

Annabelle shuffled on her knees to face her father, hands clasped together like a woman at prayer.

"Please say I can," she pleaded, even letting some tears well up in the corners of her eyes, knowing her father could never resist.

Mr Knight looked at his wife, who nodded. "Very well then," the man conceded. "If you're sure you can handle her for that long," he added with a big grin.

Annabelle instantly jumped to her feet and hugged her parents. "*Thank you. Thank you. Thank you.*" She repeated herself, first with her uncle and then with her aunt, before rushing out of the room to oversee her luggage being taken to the carriage so they could be away as soon as possible.

Before that, though, she hurried to her bedroom to bring back yet more of her Gothic-inspired novels. Room was scarce, but she could sacrifice a pair of shoes for this important addition. Once that was accomplished, she happily let the butler load her cases onto the carriage.

She waited impatiently as her aunt and uncle said goodbye to her parents and leisurely made their way over to her.

She hastily kissed her mother's cheek and hugged her father before taking her seat. She waved out the window as the carriage started to pull away.

"Goodbye. Goodbye," she called.

"Do be good, Annabelle," her mother warned across the increasing distance.

"I will, I promise!"

The journey to Bath would consume most of the day. There was no way they would arrive before darkness fell, being as it was early winter, but Mr Daniels was certain that before midnight was an achievable goal. He'd even factored in an hour's stop at an inn halfway there.

To begin with, the stop was ordinary. The inn looked much like those Annabelle knew in Oxfordshire. A lonely carriage in the courtyard suggested it wasn't busy. As Mr Daniels arranged for food and rest for the horses, and Mrs Daniels went to powder her nose, Annabelle took advantage of their absence — she had new scenery to explore.

She walked a small way from the carriage to where she could see the English countryside spread out before her. Whilst the inn was similar to Oxford, the view it overlooked was something entirely unique.

She stood in what she called her best *brooding heroine* pose, staring thoughtfully into the distance, considering the fanciful adventures that might befall her during this holiday. She was put in mind of Susanna Smith in *The Adventurer's Granddaughter*, a whimsical offering from Miss Sparrow, about a familial pair travelling across Britain in a hot air balloon, seeing all the sights and partaking in many splendid adventures along the way.

Annabelle felt as though the whole world was at her feet. She breathed in deeply, allowing the fresh air to fill her as she considered her future.

This is your time. You can be whoever you want. There's nothing stopping you.

Her reverie was broken by the pealing shriek of Mrs Daniels. Annabelle hurried towards the inn, where the noise had come from, to learn the cause of the commotion. Her aunt was in a veritable fluster, frantically searching the halls. The older woman was so excitable that even the tight blonde curls of her coiffure bounced, twitching like stalks of grain in the wind.

"Annabelle? Annabelle! Oh, there you are, dear," she cried when she saw her niece. "You must come with me. Oh, it's the happiest thing. Come, come, I'm overjoyed."

She grabbed Annabelle by the wrist, and the girl had no

choice but to follow as she was dragged through the hallways and brought to a stop in front of a woman and two girls, who, from appearances, were a mother and her daughters. There was a striking family resemblance in the brown hue of their hair, their small turned-up noses, and the extra height with which they towered over those around them.

"Here we are, you see," Mrs Daniels exclaimed, as if this explained everything.

Annabelle stood silently for a moment — a polite, if somewhat awkward, smile curled her lips. She had no idea who was standing in front of her. Was she supposed to? Perhaps she'd met them when she was younger and didn't recognise them? All she could do was wait for her aunt to make the necessary introductions.

"Oh yes, of course, how silly of me," Mrs Daniels chattered. "Annabelle, this is Mrs Evans, an old school friend of mine. We haven't seen each other for many years now. She moved to Wales, you see. Anyway, here she is, isn't it wonderful!" She paused briefly, giving Annabelle a chance to take in what she'd said before she launched into more rapid, rambling introductions.

"Mrs Evans, this is my niece, Miss Annabelle Knight. Well, she's not exactly my niece. My husband is her maternal uncle. You know what I mean. Anyway, Annabelle is accompanying us to Bath for the season."

"Oh! How wonderful," Mrs Evans cried loudly, turning to her daughters. "Look, girls, how sweet she is. How lovely, look at her curls. Oh, just darling." She didn't pause for breath, reaching out and grabbing a ringlet of Annabelle's hair. Mrs Evans' tone was the kind one might adopt with regard to a small puppy, which, to these large women, was the way Annabelle must have seemed. They were practically as wide as they were tall, and they loomed over Annabelle. The girl let out a small, nervous laugh.

Oblivious to Annabelle's discomfort, the ladies continued with their assessment. Mrs Evans' daughters, who had been tittering behind her, giggled at their mother's appraisal and added their own.

"Just wonderful," said one.

"So darling," chimed in the other. They both regarded Annabelle with the same shrewd eye with which one would appraise cattle at a market.

While the girls had clearly inherited their looks from their mother, from the brown eyes to the light dusting of freckles over their noses, their accents most definitely came from a Welsh father. It was strong and thick. Annabelle had never heard anything like it, and it took her a considerable amount of concentration to discern what they were saying.

Their mother spoke with a softer English accent that was peppered with small Welsh moments, indicating a good amount of time spent in the country. "These are my twins," Mrs Evans announced. "Carys." She gestured to the girl on her left. "And Gwennyth." She motioned to the other. Annabelle wondered how she was going to remember which twin was which. They were identical, even, unhelpfully, down to their choice in clothing. Both girls dutifully curtseyed.

One of them leant forward and added, "Most people just call me Gwen."

Right. Annabelle noted. *So Gwen is the one with the beauty spot beside her right eye.* She curtseyed again to each girl as she searched for other unique identifiers.

"Don't you just love Bath, Miss Knight?" Carys asked as though she thought every young lady in the world should have an intimate knowledge of the place.

"Actually, this is my first time," Annabelle admitted timorously.

The twins looked at each other in horror.

"Your first time!" Carys exclaimed, completely aghast, her

tone bordering on offended.

"We go every year," Gwen continued, shocked.

"It's just the best place."

"Oh, the very best!"

"Especially for eligible young ladies." At this, both girls dissolved into giggles, laughing at their own insinuations.

Annabelle nodded along, though she couldn't truly empathise. She knew that Bath was, aside from London, the best place for a young woman to be. But her parents had strictly forbidden her to travel there until she attained the age of eighteen because of its less than sparkling reputation.

"I can't believe you've never visited," Carys said contemptuously.

"How is that possible?" Gwen questioned.

Annabelle made the quick assessment that Gwen was definitely the *nicer* twin. While that didn't help her immediately, knowing that would help her distinguish which one was speaking.

"I've never had the opportunity to go before now," Annabelle replied simply. "It's something I've always wanted to do. I'm very excited to be visiting. I've read everything about it. There are so many things I would like to do while I'm there."

Gwen seemed satisfied with the answer, though Carys looked more sceptical. Suddenly, the sterner twin was seized by an idea, or at least Annabelle hoped she was — that, or she was having a fit. Carys turned to her sister and began to whisper theatrically. More giggling ensued, and they finally faced Annabelle.

"We have decided," one twin — Carys? — said, with much grandeur.

"That, as it's your first time in Bath . . ." the other added.

"And you'll need someone to show you around . . ."

"And we've been many times before . . ."

"We are the best people . . ."

"To take you under our wings . . ."

"And show you how to do Bath." They nodded in unison and eagerly awaited Annabelle's reply.

Annabelle was so confused by all the sentence-sharing and the back and forth that all she could do was smile weakly and say thank you, though she didn't know exactly what she'd agreed to.

"What a clever idea," Mrs Evans exclaimed, reminding the young girls of her existence. "Don't you think, Moira?"

"Marvellous." Mrs Daniels nodded. "Of course, Colin and I know the area substantially," she added quickly. "We know it better than anyone, but I'm sure Annabelle would prefer some younger companions to keep her company. Though, of course, she adores us. Don't you dear?"

Annabelle nodded vigorously. Her aunt didn't like to be contradicted and hated even the remotest implication that she wasn't the best at everything.

"Well then, it's settled," Mrs Evans beamed. "Girls, tell Miss Annabelle about the ball."

In the deserted inn, it wasn't difficult for the young ladies to find an empty table. Once they were sat down, Gwen began to tell Annabelle about the upcoming event.

"Oh, it *is* the best ball," she announced, her boundless enthusiasm giving away her identity. "They have it every year and it is the most *wonderful* thing. There's tea, and dancing, and card tables, and so many eligible bachelors." Gwen began to giggle girlishly then stopped suddenly. "I know!" she declared. "We must all get ready for it together. Where are you staying? You may be closer than we are."

"I think my uncle said it was St James' Square," Annabelle replied when Gwen stopped to draw breath.

Carys looked disdainful. "Hmm . . ." She paused, her nose turning up at the thought. "It *is* closer to the ballrooms, but

I'm sure it's nowhere near as comfortable as *our* accommodation in Sidney Place."

Annabelle quickly decided that arguing with Carys would be a bad choice and instead nodded her head in agreement. "I'm sure." she said sweetly. "But we risk less damage to our dresses if we are closer to the halls."

Gwen's head bobbed enthusiastically. "Quite so. And" — she spun on her toes to face Carys — "St James' Square *is* rather lovely."

The other twin gave no response to this. Instead, she raked her gaze over Annabelle's appearance. "What will you wear?" she asked in a belittling tone.

"Well, I have one dress that's my favourite. I've worn it for years," Annabelle replied fondly. "It's yellow with — "

"*That* will never do," Carys cut in harshly. "This is *the* ball of the season, you know. You can't go in wearing old clothes!" She said this with such a tone one would have thought Annabelle had suggested she would make an appearance wearing just her under-things.

Annabelle was too stunned to make an intelligible reply. Luckily, she was saved from having to find a rebuttal by the arrival of Mr Daniels.

"There you two are. I've been searching for you. Bath is still a fair way away, and we really should get going."

Annabelle nodded and rose from the table, happy to escape this odd, insulting conversation. As she left, Carys fired her parting shot.

"Don't worry," the Welsh girl called out. "We'll look through your clothes to find the least terrible gown. And if there's nothing suitable, I'm sure Gwen has *some*thing you can borrow."

Annabelle curtseyed politely and followed her uncle out of the room, trying to stop the flush she felt rising in her cheeks. She sat in solitary embarrassment whilst her aunt bid farewell to Mrs Evans and they made plans to meet for lunch the next day.

Annabelle waved from the carriage as the Evanses shrank into the distance, but as she sat back in her seat, once they'd completely disappeared, she wondered just exactly what her aunt's introductions had gotten her into.

CHAPTER TWO

The rest of the journey to Bath was — by comparison — much more unremarkable. One long lost acquaintance reappearing was enough for this trip.

Annabelle, though, was finding joy in everything. She barely sat on her seat for the majority of the journey. Instead, she leant out of the window, trying to see everything as they trundled through the countryside.

"What is that?" she would frequently ask.

Mr Daniels always gave her an answer, but Annabelle was sure he was making it up as he went along.

"He *didn't*! Really?" she cried at one statement.

"I swear it," her uncle replied, grinning like a jester. "This is the very road that Dick Turpin took with the Gang of Gregory."

"Oh, Uncle!" Annabelle hid her giggle behind her fan, but as ever, her attention was soon captured by something else.

When they reached Bath, even though it was dark and hard to see, Annabelle was hanging out of the window trying to take in as much as she could.

Mr Daniels chuckled. "Relax, my dear. You'll have plenty of time to explore the city on our trip. Tonight, we'll settle into our accommodation. Tomorrow, I would be delighted to take you on a tour of the area. How does that sound?"

Annabelle could think of nothing better. "Oh! Yes, please!" she responded, her eyes gleaming.

"And I have no doubt," her uncle continued, "that Moira will want to take you to all the best social places. The Pump

Rooms, the Upper Rooms, the Lower Rooms. Lots of . . . rooms." He chuckled and winked at his wife. "Why, my dear, you even made arrangements to meet your friend at the Pump Rooms tomorrow, yes?"

"Quite so! Why I—"

Annabelle knew that tone and knew that her aunt wanted to begin one of her long speeches where she would talk about how wonderful she was for coming up with such an idea. Luckily, her uncle seemed to sense the same thing.

"Splendid." He quickly cut his wife off, which caused Annabelle to giggle. "Look, we're coming to St James' Square now."

Annabelle looked up at the impressive residence that would be her home for the duration of this trip. It was an imposing structure, built from the stone that made Bath famous. Timidly, she exited the carriage. As she walked towards the unfamiliar place, she was met by a very strange man.

"Evenin', Miss." He came out of the shadows and tipped his hat before he was stopped by a horrendous bout of coughing. He looked as though he'd seen better days, and Annabelle was concerned he might be a beggar.

"Good evening," Annabelle replied politely, but she couldn't hide her unease. She turned away from the man to follow her uncle, but when she reached the front door to their apartment, she saw the beggar had followed her. She whispered to Mr Daniels, who looked back. He stepped down from the front porch and jovially shook the old man's hand.

"Mr Terry! How are you, sir?"

"Can't complain," the withered man replied slowly. "I'll have 'em bring up yer stuff straight away."

Mr Daniels nodded and led Annabelle inside. "Mr Terry is the butler," he explained. "He's older than this building, I'm sure. But he does a good job. Well . . . he does *a* job."

Annabelle could hear the butler shouting outside with his

thick West Country accent, pausing to let out more loud, wrenching coughs. She said no more about, or to, Mr Terry. She did feel rather guilty for thinking him a vagabond and resolved to be extraordinarily nice when she greeted him the next morning.

By the time everything had been settled into their new accommodation, the hour had grown late. They'd successfully reached Mr Daniels' goal of arriving before midnight, though only by about an hour.

Mr Daniels offered Annabelle some food that had been readied by the staff in preparation for their arrival. She accepted a small amount. However, she didn't eat much of it. She really was too tired.

Her initial excitement was waning, and the journey was beginning to take its toll on her. She sat in an armchair in front of the fire and soon nodded off. She was startled awake when she dropped her toast into the teacup that was resting on her knee.

"Go to bed, dear," Mr Daniels advised. "You'll need your energy for tomorrow."

Annabelle agreed and began to sleepily mount the stairs. Her aunt and uncle called after her, wishing her a good sleep.

When she entered her room, Annabelle changed into her nightgown and climbed into the unfamiliar bedding.

At that moment she realised just how far she was from home. Everything looked different. Everything smelt foreign. Everything sounded strange.

Bath was a lot louder than she'd expected. Even at this late hour, she could hear people out and about, filling the night air with shouting and singing.

For the first time, her stomach curled into anxious knots, twisting away at her resolve. *You can't be nervous. This is your big adventure! There's no time for fear.*

She picked up her book, determined to inspire herself into bravery, but soon the novel rested against her chest as exhaustion won out over anxiety.

Annabelle and the Daniels' had a full itinerary the next day. Beechen Cliffs was first on the list.

They took a carriage up the hill. The city spread below them from their vantage point.

Annabelle found the view breath-taking. She'd imagined how Bath would look so many times, but this was far beyond anything she'd ever hoped for.

"It's beautiful," she whispered reverently, looking out over the cream-coloured city. "I've never seen such a wonderful place. It's easy to see why so many writers use it as a setting. It's the most romantic thing I've ever seen."

"You wait until we're down in it all," Mr Daniels suggested temptingly.

However, Annabelle gave her aunt and uncle great difficulty in getting her to move on from the Cliffs. She repeatedly asked for *just one more moment* to look at something and only finally agreed to leave with the express promise that they would return there every day of their trip.

With each new attraction, Annabelle's attention was completely diverted, and everything she saw was the best of that thing she'd ever seen.

She was also excited to see the city that had inspired so many writers, such as Fanny Sparrow, who liked to use the bustling streets as a setting.

When they arrived at 5 Sidney Place, the address the Evanses had given them, they were informed the family had already left for the day.

"We'll see them at the Pump Rooms," Mrs Daniels said cheerfully.

As she walked about the city, Annabelle noticed that everybody was dressed very fashionably, just as Carys had mentioned. She looked down at herself. She was wearing a plain brown dress that was a few years old, at least. She nervously picked at her clothing, attempting to smooth out parts and hide the worst of it.

Her uncle must have noticed her fixing her appearance in the reflection of a fountain. He put a hand on her shoulder.

"You look fine," he assured her.

She looked up at him doubtingly. "Miss Evans said my clothes are too old for Bath. I don't want to embarrass myself, or you." She began picking at a loose thread on her sleeve, wishing she could pull the whole thing away and reveal a new, exciting outfit underneath.

"Yes . . ." Mr Daniels answered with annoyance. "I wondered what that comment was about when we left them. But let me assure you, you look lovely."

Annabelle's look clearly let him know she knew he was only saying that to be kind.

He sighed. "Well. It's clearly important to you, and I'd hate for you not to enjoy this trip over something as trivial as clothing. I would be happy to have your aunt take you to a seamstress, to have a new dress made. As fun as I'm sure it is to share fashion with your girlfriends, those Evans girls were twice as tall as you. And twice as wide! You'd be better off in a bed sheet than one of their dresses."

Annabelle's eyes lit up. "Really?" she asked excitedly, images of the many beautiful displays they'd passed on their walk flashed through mind. "Although my parents did give me some money before I came away, I'd hate to think of you spending yours unnecessarily."

"Nonsense," her uncle replied. "It's no more than I did for your sisters. It's only fair."

Annabelle remembered Agatha and Mary returning from their respective eighteenth birthday trips with the Daniels', showing off their new clothes and parading through the house in their exquisite attire. Annabelle had been enormously jealous and was only able to continue as she always had by knowing she would receive her own trip one day.

Then a thought occurred to her and her smile dropped. "But nowhere will we be able to have a dress ready for this evening." Her excitement left in a rush.

"We can only ask." He smiled in encouragement. "After lunch we'll go to the dress shop."

Annabelle hugged her uncle tightly, thanking him over and over. Then she ran off to find her aunt to tell her the exciting news. Mrs Daniels was trying to find the Evanses, who had promised her they would meet for lunch.

As they waited for their companions, Mrs Daniels informed Annabelle that the Pump Rooms were the social heart of Bath.

Annabelle stood with her in the atrium of the grand hall, trying to keep out of the way of the mass of people greeting friends, chatting and eating, all the while trying to stay visible for the Evanses. Visitors to the Abbey, which lay no more than thirty steps away, mingled with those who were going to tea, and the overall effect was similar to that of a cattle market.

"It is *the* place to see people and be seen," her aunt remarked. Annabelle wondered how anyone could see *anyone* in the mad bustle of the crowds.

The older lady was checking the lists of arrivals and happily clucked her tongue at the line-up. "Mrs Daverish throws the *best* parties." She pointed out a name on the list to Annabelle. "We'll be sure to get an invitation," she added proudly.

They didn't have to wait much longer for the Evanses to arrive. Annabelle heard the twins coming long before she saw them, their raucous laughter chasing around the corner ahead of them.

"I trust you had a pleasant journey," Mrs Evans opined as she came towards Annabelle's group. "Ours was *diabolical*.

Halfway here, a carriage wheel came off and we were sent *into a ditch*. The driver was completely useless, and we had to wait *far* too long to be back on the road again. But here we are!"

As Mrs Evans wove her tale of hardship, Annabelle saw Carys lean in and whisper in her twin's ear. Annabelle was sure it was Carys, because the only thing different about these identical twins was their resting expression. Carys always had a general look of disgust about her, whilst Gwen wore a kinder, gentler expression. Gwen offered Annabelle a warm smile, but Annabelle noticed the second twin laughed with her sister as they found a table for lunch.

Annabelle wrapped her arms around herself, discomfited. *Just wait until I have my new dress. Let them laugh then!*

"So," Mrs Evans babbled as they all sat down to take tea. "What are your plans for the rest of today? Excluding the ball, of course."

"Well," Mrs Daniels said as she sipped her drink. "Colin suggested we take Annabelle dress shopping."

Carys looked at Annabelle with a knowing, smug grin.

"Can we come?" Gwen practically shouted with excitement. "We know the best places and I have so many fashion plates, I know exactly what to look for."

Mr Daniels looked to Annabelle, seeking her permission. Not wanting to upset her aunt, she agreed.

"Of course," Mr Daniels said plainly, "once we have finished lunch, we shall all go together."

Four times they visited dress shops. And three times, they were refused. They were told unequivocally dresses could *not* be made in an afternoon. The third dressmaker had openly laughed in their faces at the request.

By the time they entered the fourth shop, Annabelle was feeling miserable. She asked her uncle—her aunt was busy with Mrs Evans—to speak to the shop assistant so she didn't have to face disappointment once again.

Annabelle's glum attitude didn't stop the twins almost splitting her in two as they pulled her in every direction to admire anything they deemed worthy of attention.

"What lovely ribbon," Gwen cried, dangling a gaudy strip of orange material in Annabelle's face.

"There's some positively gorgeous lace here," Carys announced a moment later.

"This would make the best reticule."

"Oh, the *best!*"

"Just look at this trim."

Annabelle once again found herself drowning in the back and forth between the sisters, not knowing who to answer first. Not that either girl paused long enough for her to be able to.

Roll upon roll of silk, muslin, and satin were pulled out, appraised, held up against Annabelle's face and unceremoniously shoved back. Annabelle tried numerous times to remind them they weren't looking to have a brand new dress made, they needed something that would be ready for that night, but they carried on as though they had all the time — and money — in the world.

"The hard part," Carys announced bluntly, stalking around the specimen dresses, "is finding something to go with your hair."

Annabelle self-consciously tucked a curl behind her ear.

"Oh, it's lovely to be sure," Gwen chimed in kindly. "It's just a difficult colour to work with."

Annabelle was always receiving comments about her hair, ever since she was small. Her mother would assure her that her auburn curls were beautiful, but for some reason, there was something about her red hair that a large portion of people seemed to have a problem with. Her mother, though, with a neat head of blonde hair, could never really understand Annabelle's trouble. Her sisters, too, were blessed with a common hair colour. Only her father really knew the problems having ginger hair created, but he had long since learnt how to shut it all out.

She caught the eye of her uncle and sent him a desperate look, signalling for help. He came directly with a large smile.

"We are in luck," he told her happily. "It seems that a young woman no longer wants a dress she had made—she wants an entirely different cut apparently. The assistant is happy to let you try it on. She said it'd be a shame to see such good work go to waste."

Annabelle jumped excitedly. "Can I see it?"

The dress was a cream muslin with flowery detail and a green sash. Annabelle adored it.

"It will do," Carys commented in a bored tone "At least it's not hideous."

Annabelle grimaced in embarrassment as Carys said this right in front of the clerk who began taking it down from the mannequin.

"I love it," she contradicted happily.

The assistant took Annabelle through to the back room for a fitting.

"I can't guarantee it will be a perfect size, of course," she commented as Annabelle stepped into the muslin dress "But happily, the woman who ordered it was quite large. It's always easier to make something smaller than the other way around. It shouldn't take too long to make the alterations."

The dress hung on Annabelle like a bedsheet, and the seamstress assistant hummed to herself as she pinned the fabric to make it a better fit. When that was done, she folded the dress and placed it in a workbench, then followed Annabelle back out onto the main shop floor.

"We'll have it ready by this evening. If you leave us an address, we'll deliver it."

Mr Daniels stepped forward, wrote out the address for

their lodgings, and agreed that the dress would be paid for on delivery.

Annabelle hugged her uncle gratefully and left the shop in high spirits. She happily told her aunt about her new purchase.

"I think I will go home and wait for the delivery," Mrs Daniels announced. "I'm feeling greatly fatigued and wish to rest before the ball tonight."

Mrs Evans expressed a desire to accompany her, and Mr Daniels chose to go with the ladies. But Annabelle wasn't ready to return to the house just yet.

"She may accompany us to Parade Gardens," Carys offered, as though she were conferring the greatest favour in the world.

"You can trust us to look after her," Gwen added.

Annabelle had discovered that the twins were only two years older than her, but from their size, anyone would be forgiven for thinking they were much older. And because of this disparity, Carys and Gwen rather talked down to Annabelle, treating her as child-like, even doll-like.

Mr Daniels gave the idea serious thought. "As long as you are back by five o'clock. And you must go straight there and straight back."

Annabelle knew her uncle's concern wasn't about trusting *her*, but rather his wariness of others, especially those in Bath. He'd made a solemn promise to her parents to keep her safe.

"Of course," Annabelle agreed happily. She gave him a kiss on the cheek and ran down the road after the twins, who'd already begun to leave.

"Have you ever been to a pleasure garden?" Gwen asked conversationally as they walked.

Once again, Annabelle was abashed by her limited experiences when Carys sniggered at her negative response.

"It's unlike anything you've ever seen," Gwen assured her.

"Look!" She pointed to a wall next to a little guard's hut. Annabelle leant against the brick, standing on her tiptoes to lie across the top as she gazed down at the garden.

The grounds were incredible. They spread out in a great wide oval on the banks of the river. A pathway wove its way through short-cut grass and perennial bushes. Bright and colourful, even in this mid-winter weather, red holly berries dotted the foliage like little earrings and the odd flower peeked out from beneath the deep green. The tall trees acted as the perfect frame for the beautiful garden against the afternoon sky—beautiful space, and very romantic. She imagined it as the perfect setting for some of the scenes in Fanny Sparrow's novels.

"This could be the very spot where Francis proposed to Miriam in *The Blooming of Miss Petunia*," she commented to herself as she ran her fingers across a purple-flowered bush.

Hearing a loud squeal from Gwen, she turned anxiously to the girl. "Whatever is the matter?" she asked, keeping a wary eye out for any wriggling insects.

"You like Fanny Sparrow?" Gwen responded animatedly, "I do, too. We both do." Gwen motioned to include Carys in the conversation. "Don't you just *love* her stories? Oh, do tell me which your favourite is. I'm particularly fond of *Making Waves with Mariah Keeper*. Oh! But what do you think will happen in the next instalment of *The Herculean Trials of Lord Lottering*? I cannot see how he will get out of that scrape! Isn't *The Mystical Miss Mapleton* simply the best thing you ever read?"

The rest of their time spent at the gardens was taken up with discussing the books in detail. However, it quickly became evident to Annabelle that Carys hadn't read as much as the other girls, and she struck Annabelle as the type of girl who preferred to be the centre of attention. After an hour of in-depth discussion, the nonparticipating twin abruptly stood up, disrupting the debate on Marco's secret messages in *The*

Literary Lover, and declared she needed to move about.

"I'm a very active person," she announced. "I can't abide sitting still and talking for too long. I *must* be in motion." She tapped her foot impatiently, clearly waiting for the other two to acquiesce to her wishes and move. Annabelle was quite happy with her current occupation, but she decided it would be better not to get into an argument with Carys.

The girls consented to leave the gardens. The sky above the city had taken on a menacing look as the clouds rolled in, thick and grey, blocking any daylight from reaching the city. They agreed they would prefer to be under the protection of the abbey should it begin to rain. They'd just made it inside the alcove when a deluge poured down, drenching any and all who hadn't taken cover.

Whilst Carys and Gwen lingered by the door to keep an eye on the weather, Annabelle was entranced by the majesty of her surroundings. The abbey was yet another of the Bath attractions that left her stunned. Who knew that one city could hold this much glory?

She stared up at the high ceiling that seemingly tried to reach the heavens. She stood in silent awe for quite some time, watching the scenes play out across the stained-glass windows, marvelling at the designs. She watched as kings were coroneted and saints were tested, joyous events and sad moments forever captured in brightly coloured glass.

What seemed like mere seconds later to Annabelle, Carys called to her.

"Hurry up! The rain's stopped. We should be getting to St James' Square. The ball is only four hours away!"

Gwen linked arms with Annabelle, and the two girls followed Carys' determined stomping through the wet streets. As they walked and dodged splashes from passing carriages, they discussed the upcoming ball.

"Is this your first ball, Annabelle?" Gwen asked. Annabelle

thought she looked comical as she tried to daintily leap over puddles, holding her skirts scandalously above her ankles.

"In Bath, yes." Annabelle tried not to become discouraged that the twins thought she was so uncultured and inexperienced that she'd never been to a ball before.

"Well, you've never been to a *real* ball until you've been to one in Bath," Carys commented haughtily.

"Definitely," Gwen agreed, once again parroting her sister.

"It'll be like nothing you've ever seen," Carys continued. Her superior tone made Annabelle feel nervous, but she was coming to anticipate the snide remarks, and each one affected her a little less.

"Don't worry, though," Gwen added hastily, as if sensing her distress. "We'll be there to help you."

"To show you what to do," condescended Carys.

Annabelle smiled weakly, and they continued in silence for a while.

They continued up the slope towards St James' Square, making their way up Milsom Street, past the rows of shops and their occupants. People were cautiously poking their heads out to check if it was still raining. As they neared the top of the street, Gwen suddenly stopped, and, as her arm was linked with Annabelle's, the poor girl nearly ran into her.

"Gregory!" Gwen announced loudly, excitedly pulling on Annabelle's arm. Annabelle began looking around, expecting to see someone. "Oh, Annabelle. You'll meet Gregory!" Gwen expanded on her sudden outburst.

"Gregory?" Annabelle asked, more than a little bewildered.

Carys supplied an explanation. "Gregory is our cousin," she clarified, in a slightly bored tone. "He'll be at the ball tonight. My sister's hoping you'll be able to meet him there." Annabelle couldn't decipher whether Carys was happy about this or not. Gwen, however, launched into a praiseful description of him.

She continued her narrative, detailing his person and personality, as they wove through the wide circle of the Circus, the elaborate stonework offering more intrigue and history, and then along the curve of houses at the Crescent. She was proudly telling Annabelle of Gregory's service in the militia as they came upon St James' Square. By the time they returned to the house, Annabelle knew nearly everything about him, except for his shoe size.

They entered the house and announced themselves to the older ladies, who happily informed Annabelle her new dress was awaiting her in her room. She ran off in girlish excitement to prepare for the ball.

CHAPTER THREE

Carys' prediction had been right. The ball truly was like nothing Annabelle had ever witnessed — astounding, loud, and oh so busy. It was certainly more lavish and well attended than any ball she'd been to at home.

It was also a lot less personal than Annabelle was used to. She'd been hoping for something more akin to her novels.

The room would go silent. All eyes would be on her.

"Who is she?" all the ladies would whisper with astonishment.

Men would trip all over themselves to ask her for a place on her dance card.

In actuality, men were indeed tripping, but only because so many people were trying to go in so many directions with no regard for anyone but themselves. Annabelle cast her gaze around the room, searching for a safe place to stand, somewhere out of the way of the heavy mass of ball attendees. She felt a rush of nostalgia for the comparatively sparse balls in her hometown.

I shall never meet the love of my life if he can't see me.

Mr Daniels bid the ladies adieu. He usually preferred to search out the card tables when attending a ball rather than participate in any dancing.

"You have a wonderful time," he said to Annabelle. He left an affectionate kiss in the air above her head, being under strict instructions from his wife not to damage any of the hard work that had gone into her hair. Then after some pushing and shoving of other guests, he was gone.

Mrs Daniels and her companion were not far behind him,

26

in search of the tearoom, leaving Annabelle, Carys, and Gwen to find their own amusement. Annabelle pressed herself against the nearest wall, trying to see the way to the dance floor. The room was heating up with the addition of yet more people, and she felt as though she was being crushed.

Beside her, Gwen and Carys were trying to catch the eyes of any available gentlemen, and they weren't completely unsuccessful. Annabelle watched as two or three gentlemen signed the girls' dance cards. Nobody seemed to be asking her, though.

"Ghastly, isn't it?" She jumped back at the sudden noise in her ear and knocked into Gwen who turned to see what was wrong. A joyful smile of realisation spread across Gwen's face, and Annabelle watched her throw her arms around the stranger.

In due course, after much hugging and delighted squealing from Gwen, Annabelle was introduced to Lieutenant Gregory Evans.

"Though it won't be Lieutenant for much longer," he added haughtily. "I'm due a promotion any day now."

Annabelle curtseyed politely. Mr Evans kissed her hand before turning back to his cousin so they could talk properly and inform each other of everything that had happened since their last meeting. Annabelle noticed that Carys stood rigidly, her arms folded across her chest and her gaze disinterested. And Mr Evans was just as cold towards the icier twin. Annabelle would've gone so far as to say that neither particularly liked the other.

She didn't really know what to make of Evans herself. He was loud and brash and quite imposing. He was no taller than she was, a dwarf compared to his cousins, but he was just as wide as the girls, and his bombastic personality made Annabelle feel very small.

She stayed quiet as the cousins conversed. She was called

upon occasionally to give her input, though it was often only a formality. Most of the time they spoke in hushed whispers, the odd glances they gave her suggesting to Annabelle that she was the topic of their discussion.

Annabelle found herself quite relieved when the first dance was called. Gwen and Carys attached themselves to the first gentlemen on their lists and Mr Evans turned to Annabelle. He flashed her what she supposed he thought was a dashing smile and grabbed her blank dance card

"Oh, all right," he said playfully. "I'll dance with you. It's a shame to see a young woman with no partners, and I'm sure it will make my cousins happy." He took her arm, even though she hadn't really consented to his offer. "I'm not usually bothered with *their* friends," he continued. "But you're not so bad." Giving insulting compliments seemed to be an Evans family trait, just as much as the brown curls, but Annabelle had grown used to it and managed to shrug it off.

She also wondered what Gwen and Carys had been saying about her that could be the cause of such *praise*.

Mr Evans led her to the dance floor, where they took their position amongst the other couples, ready to start the country dancing. Thus began the longest dance of Annabelle's life.

When the dancing finally ended, Annabelle felt a wave of relief. And she was sure several of the people around them held similar sentiments.

Gregory Evans had a peculiar dance style that relied on enthusiasm more than correct steps. Annabelle found him to be a most uncomfortable partner. Not only did he lack any grace, he'd trodden on her toes a number of times, and had sent them both spinning into the other members of their set.

And his dance-time conversation was no better. He'd spoken of nothing but himself for the duration of the dance, bragging about his connections in Bath and what an amazing place

Wales was.

"I'm stationed in England," he commented. "But of course I would much prefer to be in Wales. They just know we Welshmen make better fighters, and those impuissant Englishmen need all the help they can get!"

Finally, he'd uttered, "You know, for an English girl, you're not half bad."

Annabelle decided she'd had enough. She couldn't do this, regardless of any friendship with his cousins.

"What damn good fun," her partner exclaimed, as the music came to an end, his colourful language drawing more than a few looks from the other dancers. "What's say we do it again?" he asked, clearly oblivious to his partner's discomfort.

Annabelle couldn't bear another dance with him. Not for all the novels in England.

"I'd love to . . ." she said slowly. "But I'm desperate for a drink, do excuse me."

"I'll fetch it for you," he cried, clearly not taking the hint.

Annabelle wondered if the man had ever considered work in the theatre, as he always spoke with such drama.

"Please," she interjected hurriedly. "That won't be necessary. You're having such fun dancing, I'd hate for you to miss anything." Before he had a chance to reply, she turned and all but ran to the punch bar.

By now, the ballroom had reached maximum capacity. For the first time, Annabelle was glad of the horde, hoping to use it to her advantage to lose Mr Evans as she merged with the throng.

"Annabelle?"

She heard her name shouted in that thick Welsh drawl and briefly turned to see the man's head pop up above the sea of revellers in search of her. She quickened her pace.

She was in such a hurry to get away that it wasn't until she came face-to-face with his chest that she noticed the young man who stood in her path. She hadn't seen him before in the dance hall—she was sure she would have remembered such a face.

"I'm so sorry," she spluttered. "Do excuse me . . . I didn't see . . . in a hurry . . . I'm sorry." She was faintly aware Evans was still calling for her. His strong accent boomed across the hall, producing all number of strange looks. She glanced back to see the distance between them diminish. The gentleman-slash-obstacle chuckled.

"It's quite all right," he assured her. He was still holding onto her upper arms where he'd grabbed her to stop her from falling. "Are you Annabelle?" he asked calmly. "Because I believe that young man is trying to find you."

"Yes," she admitted with a sigh. "Though I wish he wouldn't."

"I see," the gentleman murmured. He cast a look at the man pursuing Annabelle, recognition flashing in his eyes. As Evans approached, the same recognition was echoed in his expression.

"Hartley!" Evans barked. "I didn't expect to see you here. Is your brother about?" The gentleman—apparently named Hartley—replied that he wasn't, so Evans continued. "While it's good to see you, I suppose, I can't stay to talk. I'm on the hunt, you see."

Annabelle cringed at the suggestion in his voice. He clearly hadn't noticed her, even though she stood right in front of him.

"Actually, maybe you can help me, Hartley. I'm looking for a young lady."

Annabelle, by Hartley's side, gave a gentle cough.

Evans did a comical double take as he finally noticed her. "Annabelle?" He baulked. He cleared his throat awkwardly, casting his glance to her then to Hartley and back again. "I didn't realise the two of you were acquainted." His voice held a hint of accusation and no small amount of possessiveness. He looked disgusted by the idea.

Annabelle dropped her gaze to the floor, hoping if she stared at it hard enough, it might open up and swallow her.

Yes," Hartley replied coolly. "We were just introduced, as it happens. And to that end" — he added before Evans could interject — "may I have the pleasure of the next dance, my lady?" He gave Annabelle a smile so bright the force could've knocked her from her feet.

"Well, actually, I'd rather hoped to — "

"I'd be delighted." Annabelle's swift reply stopped Evans in mid-objection. She took the arm Hartley offered her and they made their way to the dance floor.

Once out of earshot of Mr Evans, Annabelle whispered to her partner, "But we were never introduced."

The gentleman laughed softly. "But we *were*, dear Miss Annabelle."

"I don't see how," she argued. "The master of ceremonies never — "

"What are the two ways that a pair may be introduced?" Hartley asked, his voice teasing as he gently cut her off. "One, as you say, is through the master of ceremonies. The other," he continued, in an amused tone, "is through a mutual acquaintance. And was it not an acquaintance mutual to us both — Mr Evans — who said my name in front of you and yours in front of me, thereby acquainting us with each other?" He finished his explanation with a playful smirk.

Annabelle laughed and nodded, happy with his logic, and gladly followed her rescuer to the dance floor.

They were the last couple to join the set, and once they'd taken their positions, the music started.

They were to do the quadrille, a dance Annabelle enjoyed but wasn't expert at.

"I fear, sir, that this dance will give me a bad reputation as a dance partner. While I enjoy it, I have never mastered it. Will you forgive me if I step on your toes at any point?"

Hartley smiled beamingly. "Only if you promise to forgive me if I do. Though, I have *some* skill with this dance. Just follow me and I think we will be able to get through this without significant injury to ourselves or anyone else."

Annabelle thought ruefully of the poor woman Mr Evans had elbowed during their dances, who was now going to be sporting a rather large bruise on her shoulder.

"Now, may I assume," Hartley started as the dancing began, drawing her attention back to him, "that Annabelle is your last name, or is Mr Evans a familiar acquaintance of yours?" Annabelle had to wait a moment to answer, as she was twirled beneath the arm of the man next to her. But when she did reply, it was unequivocal.

"No, it isn't. And no, he isn't," she answered. "My family name is Knight. Annabelle is my Christian name. Mr Evans I only met tonight, though I am friends with his cousins. They call me Annabelle and he assumed he had permission to do the same. I don't feel comfortable with him calling me by my Christian name, but he was so confident that I didn't feel I could say anything."

"Yes, he rather does have that effect on people."

Annabelle felt quite flustered talking about Mr Evans, but if it meant Mr Hartley would continue to say her name, then she might be able to bear it. He had a clipped, neutral accent that suggested its owner was accustomed to public speaking. His voice was warm and gentle, a complete opposite to the percussive nature of Mr Evans.

There were in fact, many differences between this new gentleman and the Welshman. Superficially, they were quite the contrast—where Mr Evans was short and wide, Mr Hartley was tall and lean. He had a thin face, framed by black hair, and his skin was devoid of the cluster of freckles that were spattered across the other man's nose. His eyes were different too. On the surface, they both had blue eyes, as she did, but their different personalities produced a strong impact on their appearance.

Deeper than that, both men made Annabelle feel nervous, but for wholly disparate reasons. With Mr Hartley, it was an excited nervousness, the same as she would get from reading the more scandalous parts of a Fanny Sparrow novel. With Mr Evans, it was just a general nervousness, a feeling that something was going to go drastically and calamitously wrong.

When Annabelle next looked up, her partner was gazing at her with a thoughtful expression, as if he were trying to understand her. He seemed quite relaxed, but there was also a hint of intrigue that made Annabelle feel as though he was trying to see all the way into her soul.

The moment lasted the length of a heartbeat, then his expression changed back to merely jovial.

"A pleasure to meet you, Miss Knight." He gently raised her gloved hands to his lips — a difficult manoeuvre while dancing — and placed a small kiss on her knuckles. "Mr Charles Hartley at your service."

"A pleasure indeed, Mr Hartley," Annabelle replied with an awkward curtsey as they moved down the set.

"Might I ask if you are new to Bath, Miss Knight?" the gentleman enquired politely.

"I am," she admitted, hoping he wouldn't be as offended as the Evanses had been.

As they continued to dance, the conversation advanced in a cheerful way.

"Are you here with family?" he continued.

"Yes, my aunt and uncle. My aunt is my chaperone this evening, though she will be spending most of the night talking to her friend, Mrs Evans."

"And where have you and your aunt and uncle come from?"

"Oxfordshire."

Mr Hartley's face lit up. "I went to university at Oxford. I loved that part of the country. I've been meaning to go back, but I never found the time. Tell me, is it as beautiful as it ever was?"

Annabelle shrugged. "It's stayed the same for as long as I've lived there." She couldn't imagine how someone would find Oxfordshire exciting when there were places like Bath to visit.

The conversation was constantly interrupted by the dance. Towards the end, Annabelle realised she'd been doing most of the talking.

"Forgive me, Mr Hartley. I fear I've been dominating the conversation. Why, I think you know my family history better than I do. Tell me about *your* family."

The gentleman's smile dropped—only for an instant, but Annabelle noticed.

"There's not much to tell," he answered at last. "I have a brother, Jasper, and a sister, Beatrice. Mr Evans served with my brother, though Jasper never really had anything nice to say about him."

Annabelle nodded. She could quite understand anybody not having a positive opinion of Mr Evans. "What about your parents?" she asked curiously.

"No longer with us," Mr Hartley said plainly. "I'd rather not talk about it."

"Of course."

The conversation dwindled, then was turned back to Annabelle and her family once more.

Either way, Annabelle was enjoying Mr Hartley's conversation much more than that of Gregory Evans. She felt as though she was being talked to, rather than talked at, and Mr

Hartley made her feel as if he actually cared about what she was saying. This wasn't a feeling she was entirely used to — in such a busy household as hers, it was often difficult to give everyone their proper attentions. She wasn't neglected, not by any stretch, but sometimes she couldn't help but feel lonely and unheard. She'd known nothing else, so she'd never been very bothered. But now, with Mr Hartley, she felt as though she was the only other person in his world, and she didn't want to give that feeling up.

Annabelle very much enjoyed the gentleman's company and would have happily spent the rest of the night dancing with him alone, if not for etiquette. Sometimes, when he would regard her in a certain way, or tease her, he cast her a beautiful smirk that left her smiling — and apologising, as she forgot the steps to the dance and ended up standing on his feet. Alas, custom dictated that only two dances were permitted between unengaged couples, and not for the first time in her life, Annabelle found herself cursing propriety and social regulation.

To her utter delight, Mr Hartley seemed just as unwilling as her to part company when the dance had ended.

"If it's not too impudent," he suggested carefully, "perhaps you might introduce me to this chaperone of yours. It's only polite that I make her acquaintance as well."

Annabelle nodded enthusiastically and led him from the dance floor.

Mrs Daniels was sitting on her own, Annabelle noticed as they approached her. "Aunt?" Annabelle said.

"There you are, dear. I've been sat here alone for ten minutes! Mrs Evans had to redo her hair — someone else was wearing hers in the *exact same style*." Mrs Daniels was clearly bored, but when she was introduced to Mr Hartley, her eyes lit up. Annabelle couldn't help feeling embarrassed at the way her aunt looked at the young man, as though he was a bull at the market fayre.

But Mr Hartley didn't seem to be bothered by the blatant, shameless appraisal. He quickly gained her acceptance with some well-worded flattery.

"Miss Knight, you told me your chaperone was your aunt. Why, this woman is hardly old enough to have a grown niece!"

"Oh!" Mrs Daniels tittered like a schoolgirl, putting a hand to her chest. "Well," she stage-whispered. "I was young when I married my husband."

"He is a very lucky man," Mr Hartley continued with sickly sweet fawning.

Annabelle couldn't help but snicker as her blushing aunt pulled the man down beside her, probably hoping he'd compliment her some more. Annabelle took the seat on the other side of Mr Hartley.

The happy party were soon joined by the Evanses.

"I definitely had the most partners," Carys was bragging loudly.

"I danced with just as many as you did," Gwen rebutted.

"Dancing with the same gentleman twice doesn't count."

"At least *you* had partners to dance with," Mr Evans said moodily, giving Mr Hartley the most awful look.

Carys seemed very interested in Mr Hartley and made great efforts to keep his attention. "Annabelle. You didn't tell us you knew the Hartleys," she sneered as she took a seat.

"I didn't before tonight. We were introduced by your cousin, in fact," she added in a rare fit of audacity. He heard Mr Hartley chuckle next to her.

Carys spluttered briefly, then huffed and set about making sure that Mr Hartley had as little chance of talking to Annabelle as possible.

This left Mr Evans with the opportunity to settle himself on the other side of Annabelle, so she had no choice but to talk to him.

"Hello, Annabelle *bach*."

Annabelle felt very uncomfortable at the sight of his sickly smile. She could see he was inebriated, as he wobbled when he walked and his breath had a strong smell of port, which she got a good nose-full of when he leant close to her to whisper that last word. She knew from friends with Welsh connections that *bach* was an endearment, but Evans was making it sound a lot more leering than it was supposed to be. "How have you enjoyed the dancing?"

"Very well, thank you." Her reply was short but polite.

Mr Evans lips curved into a smug grin. "Tell me, *cariad*, was I a better partner than Hartley?" His tone suggested he thought he knew what the answer *should* be. Annabelle winced.

What an awful question. He knows I cannot answer one way or the other without giving insult to someone. I'd rather like to wipe that smug grin from his face and tell him the truth.

"Come on," Mr Evans leered. "You can be honest. I'm sure Hartley won't mind."

"What won't I mind?" Mr Hartley asked.

"Oh, nothing, I was just asking Annabelle's opinion of something." He huffed, and Annabelle was trapped into a new conversation about the beauties of the Welsh mountains compared to English ones.

And so, even though they were sat next to each other, Annabelle and Mr Hartley were hardly able to exchange more than a word or two for the next hour.

Annabelle couldn't stop herself from stealing glances at Mr Hartley. He was an attentive conversational partner, but she noticed his polite façade sometimes slipped, and his discomfort showed. For the most part, though, he was civil and courteous.

Annabelle was relieved to see he didn't treat Carys the same way he had her. Annabelle and Mr Hartley would occasionally catch each other's attention, and the smile he would beam upon her was much brighter than the one he bestowed upon Miss Evans.

The evening eventually wound to its inevitable close. Both Mrs Evans and Mrs Daniels agreed they were too fatigued to stay any longer and sent for the carriages, not giving anybody else a choice in the matter.

Mr Hartley volunteered to escort the ladies to their carriages, as Mr Daniels was sent for from the card tables, and led with Annabelle and Mrs Daniels, whilst Mr Evans followed reluctantly with his cousins.

As he helped her into the carriage, Mr Hartley kissed Annabelle's hand.

Butterflies fluttered furiously in the young girl's stomach. Under her glove, her skin felt ablaze. "I will see you again?" she asked nervously.

"I do hope so." Mr Hartley grinned back.

Annabelle was overcome with warmth and feeling. She took her fan from her bag and furiously cooled herself once Mr Hartley was gone. She had a short while to calm herself while they waited for her uncle, and she was much more mistress of herself when he finally joined them.

"How was the ball, my dear?" Mr Daniels asked as the carriage rolled through the streets of Bath, quiet in these early hours.

Annabelle's mind raced. How could she put into words everything that had happened and everything she felt? As she battled to find an adequate word, Mr Hartley's face flashed into her mind.

"It was the best ball I have *ever* attended."

Charles Hartley watched as the carriage rolled out of sight

and let out a wistful sigh. He'd been telling the truth when he told Miss Knight he hoped he would see her again. Still staring after them, he sensed Evans turn to him. He took a deep breath and rolled his shoulders back.

"You don't think you actually have a chance, do you?" the Welshman sneered contemptuously.

Charles tried not to rise to the bait, willing himself to stay silent.

Evans apparently saw this as an invitation to continue his taunting. "Even if I hadn't gotten there first," he snapped — Charles winced at his vulgarity — "do you really think she would go for a man with a brother like yours? If she knew what the name Hartley meant around here, she'd run as far from you as she could — over the border even. I bet her aunt will tell her all about how you come from money. But you don't even have *that* anymore. The old man may have straightened out when we served together, but rumour is he's back to his old ways."

Evans smirked and made a gesture as though he was drinking, then mimed stumbling around like a puppet with its strings cut. He laughed maliciously at his own wit. But when he started to leave, Charles couldn't contain his emotions.

He reached out and grabbed the Welshman's upper arm and squeezed. "Don't you dare talk about her as though she were property," he seethed. "And my brother *may* have been a drunkard at one time, but even if he still were, he's more of a gentleman than you will ever be."

Fear flashed briefly through Evans' eyes. He regained control of himself and shrugged off Charles' grip, walking away — though with significantly less swagger than he'd displayed before.

With the pompous man gone, Charles kicked the dirt at his feet, creating a small cloud of dust which settled on his boots.

Evans might have been winding him up, but it was based in truth.

He couldn't deny that many people in the ballroom had realised who he was and passed whispered assertions secretly — but by no means inconspicuously — behind hands and fans.

It was no secret that his brother was notorious throughout Gloucestershire and Somersetshire as an alcoholic. His actions in his youth had given the family name a black mark that had taken a considerable amount of the family fortune to put right again. As Evans had stated, Jasper had reformed himself whilst serving in the army, but with the recent death of their father, Charles and his sister Beatrice knew it would take a miracle for their brother to avoid falling into old habits.

One thing he supposed he could take comfort from was Evans' insinuation that Miss Knight was unfamiliar with his family's reputation. Though, of course, given the gossiping nature of Bath-ites, he feared she wouldn't remain ignorant for long. And it might seem childish, and he knew it would do him no good, but he cared about what she thought of him.

He'd been immediately taken with her. Her beauty had bowled him over, and her whole being was bewitching. Her innocence was endearing, and her sweet facial expressions caused a warmth to spread within him.

Most importantly, she wasn't like any of the young ladies he was usually paired with, by first his father and now his brother. She wasn't of high rank or of large fortune or connection. She was kind and unassuming. From the way she behaved, he surmised she wasn't in Bath to catch a husband — she was there for the pleasure of being there. She seemed genuinely happy to attend the ball.

Perhaps it was her first season — she looked to be about seventeen or eighteen. But unlike most her age, she wasn't there with a purpose, she was just having fun. And to Charles, that was incredibly heart-warming and refreshing.

But therein lay the problem. Even if it transpired that she cared little about his brother's antics, Charles knew she was certainly not the kind of girl Jasper would approve of. Since their father's passing, Jasper had taken over as head of the household, and being himself disinclined to marry, he held great hopes for his siblings' nuptials. With all the money Jasper had spent being a steadfast supporter of nearly every brewery in England, a match with wealth was essential.

It seemed that Miss Knight's chaperone had similar thoughts. Miss Knight might not be in active pursuit of a husband, but Mrs Daniels certainly was on her behalf. She'd eyed Charles as she would a piece of material she was going to buy.

That was a look Charles knew all too well. Countless mothers had been introduced to him over the years, all of them appraising him as a potential son-in-law, or in this case nephew-in-law. The very idea irritated him greatly, but he found he could bear that better than the strange looks and whispers concerning his brother. Balls really weren't his idea of a good time.

Charles took a seat on one of the stone benches outside the hall and blew a huff of breath into the air, watching the warm curls float up away from him.

Inside, the ball was coming to a close. The music had stopped, and the din of the guests was becoming quieter as people began to leave. Charles supposed he had better go home.

Really, he'd intended to be home much earlier. He hadn't particularly wanted to come this evening, but something had persuaded him, and he could definitely say he was glad he came.

As he made his way home, walking through the quiet Bath streets, and even as he was preparing for bed, Charles couldn't get Miss Knight out of his mind. Her blues eyes looked into his whenever he blinked, the soft smell of lavender and soap lingered in his nose, the gentleness of her body ghosted against him.

Heaving a weary sigh, he determined he must put her out of his mind. Jasper would never approve of such a match, so he needed to forget about her. He was actually quite glad he'd have to leave the city for a week to collect Beatrice and bring her back to Bath. He was sure that after a week, his thoughts would no longer contain her. But at the moment, he felt a great surge of sickness to think she might find herself another young man. Charles' hands clenched reflexively, and he ground his teeth in frustration, thinking of that wonderful creature with such a cad as Mr Evans.

"No!" he demanded of himself, heedless of any servants overhearing "You must let this go. For everybody's betterment."

With as stern a talking to as he could give himself, he vowed not to think of her. But his mind wouldn't listen.

All night long he dreamt of her.

In his dream, her red hair and dazzling smile made her stand out from the usual, boring crowd of the Bath ton.

Sometimes he would go to her and take her in his arms. Other times he would watch helplessly as Evans whisked her away.

When he woke the next morning, he did not feel refreshed at all.

CHAPTER FOUR

Annabelle's dreams the night of the ball were more vivid than she'd had in a long while. She'd fallen asleep reading *Abducting Miss Abigail*, and the story merged with the events of the day as her mind tried to make sense of everything.

She was being dragged up an endless flight of stairs, her assailant's face covered. He nearly pulled her arm from her shoulder as he forced her up the steps.

He pushed her through a door into a tiny room.

Her captor was in the process of tying her to a chair when another man burst through the door – Mr Hartley, shirt billowing, sword poised, his brown eyes flashing with intent. Annabelle felt a thrill shoot through her.

Hartley launched himself across the room at the masked man, and as the fight progressed, he was revealed to be Gregory Evans in disguise!

They two men continued to scuffle over Annabelle until Evans lay unconscious at Mr Hartley's feet.

The victor rushed over and untied Annabelle. He helped her to her feet and held her against him in a dramatic gesture.

He asked her if she was all right as he tucked a strand of her hair behind her ear.

She replied that she was and thanked him very much for saving her.

"My pleasure," he purred and leaned in, capturing her lips with his.

When Annabelle woke in the morning. she swore she could feel that kiss on her lips, and the phantom touch haunted her the rest of the day.

Much to her dismay, Annabelle didn't see Mr Hartley again for a whole week after the ball. All the while, though her *time* was occupied by the Evanses, Mr Hartley occupied her *mind*.

The day after the ball was mostly spent in critical assessment of the night before. Carys and Gwen compared dance partners, both extremely proud of themselves.

"Speaking of dance partners," Gwen asked Annabelle eagerly, "how did you find Gregory?" The girl leant forward conspiratorially and whispered loudly, "He seemed *very* much taken with you."

Annabelle laughed nervously. She didn't want to offend Gwen by admitting she much preferred her second partner to her first, so she insisted Mr Evans didn't like her to *that* extent. Gwen refuted very animatedly, which ended up upsetting the teacup on her hand. As she cleaned it up, Carys added her thoughts.

"I'm just glad he's moved on from *me*," she commented haughtily. "Of course, he was devastated, but I found him not to my taste *or* rank." She straightened her posture and turned her nose up directly, addressing Annabelle. "But I'm sure he'll be perfect for *you*."

Annabelle didn't say anything at first. This constant belittling from Carys was becoming annoying. "He proposed to you?" she asked cautiously.

"Of course!" Carys snapped. "It would've pleased our parents very much, but I'm destined for better things." She sniffed proudly.

She certainly thinks a lot of her herself. I wonder if any man will ever be good enough for her.

She decided not to ask any more, knowing that once Carys started upon her favourite subject — herself — she would not stop talking for at least an hour. But this explanation did verify the air of animosity that lay between them at the ball.

"Annabelle," Gwen inquired cheerfully. "Who was the other gentleman you were sat with last night?"

"His name was Mr Hartley." Annabelle smiled at the thought of him.

Carys bristled. She seemed to be insulted by their knowing each other.

"Oh, yes," interjected Gwen excitedly. "Gregory served with a Major Hartley in the militia, was it him that you met?" she asked as her sister recovered her composure.

"No, it was his younger brother. Mr Charles Hartley." She felt heat rise up her face as she thought of the young man, wondering when she would see him again.

"Oh, the elder brother is *infinitely* more divine," Carys added quickly. The young woman seemed to be taking personal offence at Annabelle showing any happiness.

Gwen pondered for a moment. "Isn't he known for . . . drinking to excess?" She lapsed into giggles.

Annabelle wanted to ask more about that revelation, but Carys cut in before she could say anything.

"*That* doesn't signify," the more abrasive twin remarked harshly. "He's reformed after his time in the army. And besides, he's so rich, he may do as he chooses. After his father died, he inherited everything. There's a lot of money in the family. By all accounts, he's very handsome — all say much more so than his brother." She finished her speech with a glare at her sister, who immediately tried to appease her. Annabelle felt a pang of sympathy for the second sister.

"Oh, to be sure, I've heard he is handsome," Gwen joined hurriedly. "One of the most handsome men in the country. And if his drinking is reformed, well then, it's no matter at all."

"He must be exceedingly handsome indeed," Annabelle

supposed, "because I found his brother to be —"

"The brother is only a country clergyman. That's no profession for such a high family." Carys paused for a moment. "Yes," she mused in a superior fashion. "I'm glad he didn't ask *me* to dance. I most definitely would've had to decline, despite our *long* history with the family." She looked pointedly at Annabelle, finishing with, "It would've been far too awkward."

Annabelle didn't know quite how to respond. She stared into her teacup, at a loss for anywhere else to look. She was upset that Carys would speak so ill of Mr Hartley, and she had a feeling she was doing it just to argue with her.

But at the same time, she was glad to know she wasn't competing with her for Mr Hartley's attentions. She thought about how much she'd enjoyed dancing with him and promised herself that no matter what the Evanses thought, she would definitely do it again.

She happily reminisced as the conversation moved on to a new topic.

Despite the uneasiness of the friendship that had developed between Annabelle and Carys, the two families spent most of their time in each other's company, going on trips and exploring the area. Mr Daniels was adamant that Annabelle shouldn't miss out on any experiences.

Everywhere they went, Annabelle would look for Mr Hartley, and as she went longer and longer with no sight of him, she began to fear he'd left Bath for good.

She became quite miserable, and Carys thought it hilarious to tease her about his absence. An added bonus in the virulent girl's eyes was that it also annoyed Mr Evans if he happened to be within hearing.

"He must be tending to his flock. Why, he's practically a farmer." The Welsh girl would laugh maliciously. "We shall have to fit you out with a crook."

The nicer twin, Gwen, never said anything mean to Annabelle, but she would laugh whenever her sister did.

One particular trip, about a week after the first ball, saw the whole party in Corsham Court. Mr Daniels was a great admirer of the architect Capability Brown and delighted in visiting his properties. Annabelle had lost count of the times she'd been taken to Blenheim Palace as a child.

The party of the Daniels, Annabelle, and the four Evanses toured the grand house, led by the housekeeper, Mrs Prewitt. She was a knowledgeable older lady with a very sharp wit and a sharper tongue if you crossed her or touched anything you weren't supposed to.

"The master is away," the old woman informed them as she let them in.

"Pity," Annabelle overheard Carys remark to Gwen under her breath. "I hear he is quite the eligible bachelor."

"Isn't he nearly forty?" Gwen whispered back as though she were talking of someone who had committed treason.

"He can be as old as he likes," Carys replied. "The older the better, in fact. The quicker he dies, the quicker I get his money."

"Oh, Carys, you *are* dreadful." Gwen laughed.

Annabelle tried to pay no mind to the young ladies' conversation, but she did think it in very poor taste to talk so in front of his staff, particularly one such as Mrs Prewitt, who spoke so well of him.

Instead, she happily stuck to her uncle, who was like a child in a toy shop. He couldn't stop praising the architecture, pointing out every little detail to Annabelle, who listened obediently, glad to see him so happy. He even knew things the housekeeper didn't, and the two of them talked in depth about the benefits of natural parkland as opposed to formal gardens.

Carys, meanwhile, paraded around the rooms and passed judgement on everything, stating what she would do with her own house and the right amount of money.

"*I* certainly wouldn't have it like *that*."

"Oh, *that* wouldn't do."

"That would have to go *immediately*!"

Gwen would agree with her, of course, and occasionally offer her own suggestions, which were usually shot down.

"You know, Gwen," Carys remarked after a particularly contentious suggestion. "I often wonder at the miracle of us being related. Were we not identical, I might doubt it."

Annabelle heard the housekeeper murmur something about which twin she felt sorrier for having to be related to the other, and had to hide a snigger.

"I don't know why you're laughing," Carys huffed. "If you're going to marry a *clergyman*, you'll only be able to dream of this kind of luxury."

"*I* would certainly be able to give you a considerably more fashionable living," Mr Evans added self-assuredly.

He'd spent the whole trip bragging to Annabelle about his own abode and adding barbs of his own about the Hartleys.

"Indeed, the Hartleys may look wealthy, but it's all a façade. I'm sure you must've noticed how people were looking at him. It's a difficult name to be associated with. I can survive it of course, but you ..."

Annabelle tried to listen politely but found it very difficult. She never liked to speak truly ill of a person, but she found Mr Evans to be exceedingly arrogant and was enjoying his company less and less. Unfortunately, the man in question didn't seem to notice her reluctance to spend time with him and continued to seek her out

She'd thought about talking to Mr Daniels about Mr Evans, but she didn't want to make a fuss. His overconfident attentions to her were harmless, really, just annoying, and Mrs

Daniels seemed so happy Annabelle was getting along with her school-friend's family that she didn't wish to upset her aunt.

In the spirit of not making a fuss, Annabelle didn't object when Mr Evans offered her a seat in his curricle for the return journey. They were leaving early to have time to prepare for Mrs Daverish's party that evening.

It wasn't—for Annabelle at least—a pleasant journey. As soon as the group departed, Mr Evans set off at such a pace that Annabelle nearly lost her bonnet. They left the others in the party trailing behind them.

She politely declined Evans' suggestion that she hold onto him, citing a fear that any sharp turn or sudden stop would cause them both to fall off. In actuality, she really didn't want to get that close to him.

She was concentrating so hard on not losing her seat that she was unable to join in with Evans' discussion on the beauty of the Welsh countryside—not that her lack of response mattered to him, of course. As usual, he contentedly held a one-sided conversation until they arrived back in Bath. Annabelle was quite positive she'd never have to visit Wales now, she was so certain of what it looked like thanks to Evans' description.

They finally reached St. James' Square, only to find Mr Daniels' carriage already there.

"Impossible!" Mr Evans boomed indignantly.

"How so?" Mr Daniels replied calmly. When the Welshman's back was turned, he cast Annabelle a cheeky smirk.

"My curricle is the fastest in Wales! I've never been beaten in a race."

"Well, that will be what happened then," Mr Daniels continued in a cool voice. "I didn't realise it was a *race*. Therefore, I wasn't aware of the impossibility of my actions."

Annabelle tried to hide her smile behind her hand, but she

was sure she failed miserably. She rather enjoyed seeing Mr Evans challenged.

Visibly embarrassed and flustered, huffing and puffing but saying nothing, Mr Evans didn't stay much longer. He quickly left, not even waiting for the rest of his party to return. Annabelle and her uncle had a long laugh about the situation once he was gone.

To Annabelle's guilty relief, the Evans twins had decided to make themselves ready for the ball at their own rooms instead of joining Annabelle, and the girl was able to get dressed in peace.

Annabelle had chosen her favourite blue dress for the evening. Her decision had everything to do with the fact that it was a comfortable dress and most certainly had nothing to do with Mr Hartley mentioning at their acquaintance that he was particularly partial to that colour. And she definitely wasn't wishing with all her heart that he would be there.

As she dressed, she couldn't help but imagine what it would be like to see him again.

Like her novels, he would return realising how much he'd missed her and declare his love for all the world to hear. Then they would happily embrace as the surrounding throng congratulated them.

Perhaps it wouldn't happen *exactly* like that, but a girl could dream.

With little time to rest or prepare for the ball, Annabelle and the Daniels soon rushed out again to Mrs Daverish's lodgings in Camden Place.

The rooms were already quite crowded when they arrived, and after greeting Mrs Daverish, the first thing Mrs Daniels did was to seek out the Evanses. Taking Annabelle by the hand, she wove through the throng of people, calling out for her friends along the way, drawing no amount of odd looks.

At some point, though she couldn't say exactly when, Annabelle found herself separated from her aunt—she had no idea how long they hadn't been holding hands anymore. She was actually quite happy to take a deep breath and take in the atmosphere of the party. She found the whole thing quite overwhelming. She was also pleased she didn't have to deal with the Evanses immediately. She'd already had enough of them for that day, and she didn't care to hear what Carys thought was wrong with this dress, or to listen to any more disparaging remarks about clergymen.

Sadly, Annabelle's Evans-less state didn't last long. As she watched the partygoers, the cousin slunk up beside her.

"And how are we this evening, Annabelle *bach*?" he slurred, as though he hadn't seen her a mere hour earlier. He smelt strongly of whiskey and cigar smoke and didn't give Annabelle a chance to answer his question before he continued. "You know, *cariad*, I was quite hurt when Hartley stole you from me the last time we were at a ball together, I was rather enjoying your company. And I saw you first," he added childishly.

Annabelle recoiled. A shiver ran through her as Evans leant closer.

"He had no right to ask you," the Welshman drunkenly rambled. "I'll admit I was quite angry you didn't say no to him, but perhaps you felt you couldn't. Next time, say the word and I'll defend you from him." He took a step closer "But he isn't here now, is he? Some say he's completely left town. I have you all to myself." His tone was laced with both triumph and lecherous intention.

But his insinuations were lost to Annabelle because Evans was wrong—Mr Hartley *was* there. He'd just entered, looking tall and elegant and just as wonderful as she remembered. Her stomach twisted with excitement, only to drop through her feet a moment later. Mr Hartley also had a young lady on his arm! Annabelle blanched at the sight of her, beautiful and dainty, tall and graceful, making Annabelle feel decidedly inadequate.

He did mention a sister, Annabelle recollected, trying to calm her fluttering heart. *They do look similar . . . I hope.*

The pair had been detained by Mrs Daverish, and as such, they'd not seen her yet. From the looks of the conversation, they wouldn't for a while. She decided, nonetheless, that she would go to them. However, that wasn't as easy as she'd hoped. Mr Evans had still been talking while her mind raced, oblivious to her own obliviousness. She heard him talk about his skills at the card tables, then felt his hands snake around her waist.

"But I'd much rather be with you," he whispered in her ear. He pulled her close against him, so close she could feel his stale breath blow against her neck. She let out a small squeal, though nobody but Evans heard, and he let out a low chuckle. She tried to step away, but he tightened his grip and pulled her back.

"You're so pretty, *cariad*," he leered into her ear, tugging on an errant lock of her hair that had fallen out of the coiffure.

"Please, Mr Evans" — she struggled in his grip — "this isn't" — she pushed and pulled against his arms — "proper behaviour . . . for . . . a . . . party!" At the last word, she finally freed herself from his wandering hands. She stumbled forwards and nearly lost her balance.

She looked up embarrassed, hoping nobody had noticed their encounter. Luckily, most of the partygoers seemed unaware. She could, however, see Carys shake with laughter from one of the sofas. Gwen joined in, though she looked slightly more sympathetic.

Annabelle glanced around and saw Mr Hartley looking at her with no small amount of concern. She felt heat rise to her cheeks. How much had he seen? Was he concerned that she'd tripped, or concerned she was with Mr Evans?

Charles was moments away from storming across the room and giving Evans a piece of his mind.

"She's quite well," Beatrice whispered to him, putting a soothing hand on his arm. "Look, she's coming over now."

While fetching his sister from Gloucestershire, Charles had made mention of Miss Knight. Frequently. However, Beatrice, instead of affirming his assertions that Jasper would never approve, had been utterly delighted about her young brother being in love and had asked him questions nonstop for the whole trip.

Now that she was about to meet the much-described Miss Knight, Charles could feel his sister vibrate with excitement. Years of reading novels had made her a hopeless romantic.

As Beatrice had pointed out, Miss Knight was coming towards them with a determined stride. Every so often she would check behind her shoulder to see where Mr Evans was. Charles saw her shoulders physically relax when she saw he didn't follow her.

Miss Knight stopped in front of Charles and Beatrice, still looking a little flustered from her encounter with Evans. Charles noted a delightful rosy tint to her cheeks. The woman curtseyed and addressed him rather loudly.

"Mr Hartley, please forgive the impertinence, but I do believe you promised to introduce me to your sister."

Charles' stomach dropped. He had promised no such thing and could only conclude she was making up conversations in order to escape from the Evanses. He had to admit his pride was a little hurt that she didn't want to speak to him just for the sake of his company. Part of him had hoped her to exclaim in joy of his return and leave no doubt she had missed him.

Now who's the hopeless romantic?

He decided to test her, to see what she would do if he foiled her plan. He was also curious to see how she would react to him being with another woman.

"Oh, this isn't my sister," he replied aiming for cute and

teasing but he quickly saw he'd missed the mark.

"I'm–I–I'm so sorry," Miss Knight blurted in a distressed tone, her eyes darting between the two people.

He was going to apologise, but Beatrice beat him to it. "My *brother*" — the young woman dug her elbow into Charles' ribs — "thinks he's being funny. I'm Beatrice Hartley. I'm so pleased to meet you, I've heard so much about you."

Charles nearly laughed outright when Miss Knight looked panicked at the thought.

"You . . . you have?" she stammered, blushing.

God help him.

Seeing Miss Knight again ignited all of Charles' feelings. Her face seemed even more beautiful than he remembered, decorated by the blush that had been on his mind since their parting. Her gentle voice flowed like honey in his ears, more musical and sweet than any hymn. The rush of emotion caused a tightening of his body, reminding him of the times he'd awoken after dreaming of her.

Charles took a moment to recover himself. "All newcomers to the social scene must be discussed in great depth by all," he said at length before cursing internally. *Yes, Charles. Because that isn't the weakest argument she's ever heard.*

Annabelle giggled, visibly relaxing. "I'm beginning to get the impression you like teasing me, Mr Hartley," she suggested with a bright smile.

Before he could stop himself, Charles found a word leaving his mouth.

"Immensely," he told her, his voice constricted by his feelings.

The young woman laughed again, but Charles was sure he saw a flash of excitement in her eyes. He couldn't stop looking at them. Such a bright, intense blue. They matched her bubbly personality, whilst also holding a flower-like beauty that enveloped her whole being.

"Would you care to take tea with us, Miss Knight?"

Beatrice broke the momentary silence, reminding the two of them she was still there.

Charles held his breath as he waited for her to respond. Miss Knight gave the most enthusiastic consent he'd ever seen, and he felt his whole body respond. Trying to bring himself under control, he followed behind the ladies as Beatrice found them a seat.

To start with, the group covered the basic topics deemed appropriate by the laws of politeness — *how was your day? Isn't the weather fine today? I hope the journey wasn't too difficult.* Beatrice asked a lot of the same questions of Annabelle that Charles had on their first meeting, even though she knew all of the answers, having demanded them of him every waking moment.

Charles preferred to remain quiet, happy to just listen to Miss Knight speak, but Beatrice soon brought him into the conversation.

"I love those books!" — the ladies had moved onto the topic of Fanny Sparrow — "They're silly and frightfully fanciful, but I just can't put them down. Charles bought me the very first one and I've read every new one ever since. Charles has read them all himself, though he'd never admit it." She beamed teasingly at her brother.

Two could play at that game. If his sister would dare to tease him, he would certainly have to retaliate.

"I would indeed," he declared melodramatically. "Gladly. Proudly." He stood up in their corner, and cleared his throat, as if preparing to make a grand speech. This would embarrass her, teach her to tease him. "I have read every one of Fanny Sparrow's novels," he declared passionately. "And I would again." He finished with a small bow. His spectacle caused some strange looks from some of the other guests, but most were too busy with their own conversations to notice. He sat back down to rapturous laughter and playful applause from the two girls.

"It's been so wonderful here." Miss Knight grinned once their laughter had subsided. "To see the beautiful country-side, and so many gothic buildings, really changes how you read the books. Only the other day we were walking by the folly castle, and it looked for all the world like a scene from *The Shameless Sham of Samuel Shawford.*"

Charles found himself enchanted by her enthusiasm and her passion for these novels, so he hatched a plan.

"Have you visited Witches Cove yet?" he asked with a wicked smile. Annabelle vigorously shook her head, visibly excited.

"It's just beyond Clifton," he expanded. "Though I'm not surprised Mr Daniels hasn't ventured out there with such a delicate young lady—it has a very dark reputation." He affected a dramatic tone as Miss Knight sat forward in her chair.

"What happened there?" she asked, her voice barely above a whisper.

"Are you sure you want to know?" Charles teased. "It's *truly* awful." Miss Knight nodded, and he leaned in closer. "Then I shall tell you." The girl's eyes were wide, and she was already hanging on his every word. The gaze with which she looked at him set Charles' insides on fire.

"The story begins a long time ago," he began theatrically, waving his arms and hushing the laughing Beatrice. "In medieval times, three young ladies lived in a cottage on a cove not far from the village of Clifton. They weren't like the villagers, most of whom thought the ladies must be witches because they behaved so oddly.

"One day, a young rich boy suddenly broke off his engagement with a wealthy landowner's ward and ran away with the shepherd's daughter. Everybody in the village was shocked, and the young couple fled the town to avoid persecution.

"They ran into the woods and found themselves at the cottage of the three ladies. They told the ladies their story and the ladies let them stay, as long as they helped around the cottage.

"Many weeks later, a villager was hunting in the woods and spotted the young man gathering herbs by the river. He followed him back to the cottage, where he saw him give the ingredients to the three ladies who threw them into a big cauldron. He ran back to the village and told everyone what he'd seen.

"He rounded up a mob to go the cottage and attack the witches and their servants. They went out with torches and pitchforks and marched down to the cottage, where they found the ladies gathered around a fire and the young couple sweeping the floor.

"They accused the ladies of kidnapping the young man and bewitching him so he'd leave the landowner's ward. The ladies tried to say it wasn't true, but nobody believed them. They told the couple to run, and they did, into the night, never to be seen again.

"The ladies were left in the cottage, trying to convince the villagers their *potion* was just broth, but the mob wouldn't be reasoned with and, in a fit of rage, the thatch on the cottage roof was set ablaze and soon the whole building was up in flames with the poor ladies still inside.

"The local pastor condemned their souls to hell and the villagers cheered. They stayed to watch until all that was left was ash and ruins. Legend has it that to this day you can still hear the ladies crying out, and if you stand close to the ruins of the cottage, you can feel the heat of the flames." Charles finished his story and leant back in his chair, breathless from the intimacy of the moment.

Annabelle was speechless. "How wonderful," she breathed at last as if in a trance. Her tone sent pleasurable shivers through Charles' body. He was dangerously close to leaning across the table and kissing her.

Beside him, Beatrice chuckled loudly. "Wonderful?" she teased. "Those poor innocent women didn't think it wonderful, I have no doubt."

"Gosh . . . no . . . I didn't mean . . . but of course," Miss Knight gushed, her cheeks a dark red. "I meant the story, it was so wonderfully gothic, and you told it so well, Mr Hartley."

Nodding his head in thanks, Charles cast his mind back to the stories he'd read belonging to Fanny Sparrow, and which ones he would love to read to her alone.

"I shall have to ask my uncle if he will take me, it sounds wonderful," Miss Knight remarked eagerly.

"Out of the question," replied Charles sternly. That would ruin his entire plan in telling the story to begin with. "It was us that told you of it and of its history, I think it only right we be the ones to accompany you." He turned to Beatrice. "Don't you agree, dear sister?"

"Far be it for me to disagree with you my dear, *dear* brother," Beatrice answered playfully. "But in fact, I do agree. We could make a day of it. What do you say, Miss Knight, could you be prevailed upon to join us on our adventure?" She smiled warmly at the young girl.

"I'll have to check with Mr Daniels, but I'd love to," Miss Knight replied. "I'll seek him out and ask him at once." She leapt up from the table in a flurry of excitement. As she disappeared in search of her uncle, Beatrice turned to her brother.

"I like her," she stated, a smile on her face.

"Yes," said Charles thoughtfully, his body still tingling with sensation. "I rather do as well."

Chapter Five

After securing consent from her uncle, Annabelle agreed with the Hartleys to make their trip the very next day. There were no other plans that either party was aware of, so it was agreed that Mr Hartley and his sister would call early in the morning.

Mr Daniels had remarked to Annabelle that he was glad she was making some new friends. Annabelle knew he didn't have the highest opinion of the Evanses, and she'd heard him arguing with his wife about them in the parlour when they thought she was asleep.

"I don't like the way they treat her," her uncle had stated late that night.

"You don't like them being friendly?" her aunt replied sarcastically.

"*That* is not friendly. It's . . . it's . . . Well, I don't know how to describe it, but it's not friendly. That twin, Kelly? Kerrie? She's always making silly little comments at Annabelle's expense. Annabelle pretends she doesn't mind them, but I know they must be painful to her. And that *Gregory* Evans! Does he have any other topics of conversation other than himself? He's far too arrogant, in my opinion. I don't like the way he looks at her."

This annoyed Mrs Daniels so much that she stormed off to bed without another word.

Annabelle felt awful that she couldn't like her aunt's friends, but having the support of her uncle helped to assuage her guilt.

When morning broke, Annabelle sat impatiently in the parlour waiting for her companions. Mr Daniels would chuckle every now and then as her eyes raked the courtyard for any sign of a carriage, and she jumped whenever she heard a knock at a door.

"They'll be here soon," her uncle promised, mirroring her father's words when she'd been waiting for *him* to arrive.

The Hartley's carriage rolled into St James' Square a little after nine o'clock, and Annabelle rushed to greet them. She was so excited she managed to get to the door even before Mr Terry. She enthusiastically ushered the pair up to the drawing room, then dashed around, offering tea and cake.

"Annabelle, my dear," Mr Daniels called out, interrupting her mad rushing. "Aren't you going to introduce me to your friends?"

Annabelle stopped in her tracks, embarrassed at her lack of social grace. "Oh gosh . . . Of course," she spluttered. "Do forgive me." She placed the teacup in her hands on the small wooden table next to Beatrice, apologising all the way. "Uncle, may I introduce you to Mr Charles and Miss Beatrice Hartley." The relevant persons curtseyed and bowed, hands were shaken and kissed.

"Hartley . . ." Mr Daniels mused. "That's a name I know, I'm sure of it. If only I could remember how."

As he said that, Mr Hartley's demeanour changed for the worse, and Annabelle was reminded of the conversation she'd had with the Evans twins about the eldest Mr Hartley. She felt overwhelming pity for him, and for Miss Hartley too. They were the nicest people she could ever wish to meet and they were constantly marred by the actions of their brother. Annabelle sent warning looks to her uncle, but they went unneeded.

"Tell me, Mr Hartley," he said, guiding the man to the

chairs around the fireplace. "Your father was in the service, yes?"

"Yes," Charles answered eagerly, obviously relieved at the change of topic. "In his youth. General Alfred Hartley."

Annabelle tried to listen in, keeping one eye on them whilst trying to converse with Miss Hartley, who didn't seem to mind that she didn't have Annabelle's full attention. Mr Daniels didn't talk to her very much about his military days, and she was excited by the intimate connection of his having served with the Hartleys' father.

Mr Hartley stopped talking, seeming uncertain about what he would say next. His sister helped him.

"Our father died a year ago," she informed Mr Daniels gently.

"I'm sorry," the man replied, full of sincerity. "It's such a shame he and I lost touch. He left the settlement a few months before I did, and our responsibilities prevented a diligent correspondence. He was a remarkable man."

Both siblings thanked him sincerely. Then Miss Hartley put a hand on her brother's shoulder.

"Dear Charles, shall we continue on without you?" she asked, teasingly. "If we don't leave soon, we won't have enough time for anything. You are, of course, more than welcome to stay here."

Annabelle stifled a laugh as Mr Hartley rose to his feet as though the seat had stabbed him.

"No, no, I couldn't possibly leave you without a chaperone. Do you not agree, Mr Daniels?"

"Quite right," the older man agreed with a smile. "Goodness knows what trouble they could get into. Especially at Witches' Cove." He winked theatrically at Annabelle and Miss Hartley, who laughed amiably.

"Oh Uncle." Annabelle laughed. "It can't be that terrible."

"I'm sure you are right, my dear. All the same, I'm sure

young Hartley would much rather spend his days with you lovely ladies than with a doddery old fellow like me," he joked.

Mr Hartley assured him it would be a pleasure to have him with them, but the offer was graciously declined on the grounds that Mr Daniels wanted to stay at home to amuse his wife.

Mrs Daniels had been quite upset that Annabelle was going on a trip with the Hartleys and not inviting the Evanses along too. She'd been sulking in her room ever since her argument with her husband the night before.

So, Mr Daniels stood alone in the doorway and waved them off. "Have a good day, all of you. Mr Hartley, I'm trusting you with my most prized possession." His tone was mostly joking with a hint of seriousness.

"Uncle!" Annabelle cried in embarrassment.

"I will guard her with my life," Hartley replied. He offered Annabelle and Beatrice the crook of an arm each. "Ladies, let's be off." He led them out to the carriage, whereupon they bid adieu to Mr Daniels and began their adventure to Witches' Cove.

It was midday by the time they arrived in Clifton. Charles had driven slower than usual, wanting to make sure Miss Knight could take in all the sights. He felt smug happiness every time he heard her *ooh* and *ahh*.

Beatrice had prepared lunch for them all, and their first job on arrival was to eat it. They made happy conversation as they ate, Miss Knight eating very quickly because she was so excited to see the cove. Charles laughed gently as Beatrice told her to slow down.

"The cove will still be there in an hour. And we don't want to miss it because we've had to take you home with indigestion."

Charles found himself looking frequently at Miss Knight. Sometimes he would watch what she was doing, how she gracefully ate an apple or licked away stray jam. Sometimes he just looked at her, taking in her beauty. He'd looked at her face so often he was confident he could tell anyone who asked the number of freckles on her nose.

He had a chance to count her freckles even closer when they began their trek to the cove. Miss Knight got her bonnet stuck in a tree branch, and he came to her assistance. As he untangled her, he stood so close to her, he could feel her warmth, and he was pleased to find that her breathing had sped up quite considerably.

If this had been one of those novels she and his sister enjoyed so much, this would be the moment when he would lean in and grant her a kiss. His head began to swim. It would only take the smallest movement for them to be connected.

He moved slightly, resting his weight on the branch that had entrapped the bonnet. Both he and Miss Knight were silent. Though Charles was sure he wouldn't have heard her say anything anyway, so loud was his heartbeat and the blood rushing in his ears.

Miss Knight too seemed to sense that this was an extraordinary moment and watched him carefully, expectantly.

But Charles never did have the best of luck. He pushed slightly too hard on his supporting branch, and the wood snapped, sending him tumbling idiotically to the ground. Miss Knight helped him up, and though they were now even closer to each other, the moment had passed, and they joined Beatrice once more. Their adventure was resumed, and they finally reached the cove.

Charles hung back to watch Miss Knight's reactions to the site—her amazement and wonder filled his heart with a happy warmth. As he watched, the wind began to pick up, and as he pulled his coat tighter around himself, he cursed the autumn weather. Thinking about it, Charles had never been particularly fond of autumn. The weather was too changeable, going from hot to cold in an instant. But seeing Miss Knight amongst the trees, surrounded by the leaves that matched her hair, he realised it quite possibly could become his favourite season.

A rush of happiness flooded through him as he watched Miss Knight's enjoyment of Witches Cove. She reminded him of a puppy. She would run to look at something, then look back at him or come over to him, and then run off to another part.

"It's so beautiful," she sighed after a while. "Doesn't it remind you of *The Amorous Archaeologist*? I wish I could draw it, but I'm not artistic at all."

"You don't draw?" Charles asked in teasing mockery. "I thought all young ladies drew. Is it not part of being *accomplished*?"

"I had lessons as a child," Miss Knight admitted. "My mother was desperate for me to be proficient at *something*, but I just couldn't seem to manage it."

"I don't draw much either," Beatrice reassured the lady, tucking her arm into the crook of Miss Knight's. "I much prefer to admire things as they are instead of having to look for geometric patterns or wondering exactly what colour it is. What does it matter if the sky is periwinkle or powder blue? It's no less beautiful." Miss Knight nodded in agreement.

"Philistines!" Charles cried in mock exasperation. Though he considered it a fair trade, really—the idea that one who would make the most beautiful study for a drawing should have no drawing talent of her own seemed equitable. How unjust to everyone else if she was absolutely perfect.

As the afternoon wore on, Charles noticed Miss Knight seemed to be asking a lot of questions about their family. Her interest lay like a heavy stone in his belly as time and again he diverted the conversation. He knew their friendship would be ruined when she learnt of their reputation, so he wanted to enjoy the camaraderie for as long as possible.

With a deep sense of melancholia, he listened to her tell them how much she preferred their company to that of the Evanses. All he could think was that it would come to an end soon — he was already on borrowed time. They'd expected Jasper to come to them the day of the party, but as yet he hadn't appeared. This had caused a reckless rush of spontaneity in Charles, who was selfishly determined to enjoy Miss Knight for as long as he was able.

The trio began the return journey in the late afternoon, before the sun began to set. Charles was not ready for their fun to end, and before they left he petitioned Beatrice to invite Miss Knight to dinner. "It will be just about that time when we reach Bath," he argued.

"Why don't *you* ask her?" Beatrice questioned knowingly.

"It would sound better coming from you," Charles lied, trying to avoid admitting he didn't want to face the potential of being rejected.

From his riding seat, Charles heard Miss Knight consent to dinner and then converse happily with his sister. Charles' heart was warmed to see the two of them getting on so well. Though, once again, dread and doubt crept into his soul, and now a sense of shame as well. The regret would have been hard enough if it had only been *his* heart that would have been broken when Jasper forbade the relationship. Now, the guilt was infinitely worse, knowing that he would be upsetting his sister as well.

He was still debating the topic as they arrived in Bath, and that greatly affected his mood. Though not as much as the sight of a carriage outside their residence. He opened the door gingerly, waiting for Jasper to speak. His brother did not disappoint his expectations.

"Hold it right there," a loud voice boomed across the atrium. "Where in the blazes have you been?"

Whilst annoyed that his brother had now ruined his chances of enjoyment for the evening, Charles did happily receive Miss Knight when she jumped into his arms from fright when Jasper used his *commanding major* voice. With her beside him, he felt a rush of confidence, and he did something he rarely ever did.

"We could ask the same of you, Jasper," Charles replied, boldly. He heard Beatrice gasp quietly at his display of bravado. "We expected you yesterday."

Instead of answering, Jasper strode to them. Charles dropped his gaze to the ground, his earlier flash of boldness trickling away. Jasper had always been a hard person to deal with, but since becoming head of the household, he was infinitely worse.

The eldest Hartley addressed Miss Knight. "And who might you be?"

Like most people who met him, Miss Knight seemed to be intimidated by the imposing figure of his brother and remained silent.

Charles came to her rescue. "This is Miss Annabelle Knight. Miss Knight, may I present Major Jasper Hartley, our brother."

Miss Knight curtseyed politely

Charles watched as his brother assumed his superior stance. He always stood with a strong military air, even though no longer in the regiment, and he held himself with the pride of the head of a house. The only problem, as Charles saw it, was that he was in no way humble about it and held himself as though he was being perpetually followed by a bad smell. He sneered down at anyone he considered to be beneath him. Thus was his attitude towards Miss Knight, which embarrassed his siblings enormously.

"Miss Knight is staying in Bath with a Mr and Mrs Daniels, her aunt and uncle—" Beatrice began to inform him before being cut off.

"And why is that important to me?" Jasper demanded, sounding as though this was wasting his valuable time.

Charles had to exert a great deal of self-control in order not to roll his eyes at this. "Mr Daniels," Charles continued, very annoyed that his brother was treating Miss Knight and her family with such contempt. "Or Brigadier Daniels, as he once was, served with our father in Bombay, as it happens."

Major Hartley's stance changed and his demeanour followed suit. "Really?" He regarded Miss Knight with more interest.

Charles cast the young woman a look. She had every right to storm out of the house and never talk to any of them again, such was the insult Jasper had dealt her. She had such a sweet nature about her Charles was sure she'd not encountered many a person with Jasper's attitudes. He was impressed when Miss Knight instead answered his brother without flinching.

"My uncle speaks very highly of General Hartley." She gave Charles a small smile that he felt in every corner of his body.

"Of course he does," Jasper replied to Charles and Beatrice's utter horror. "Are they here for long? I suppose I should pay my respects. I'll go this evening." He called the butler for his coat before Annabelle could even answer his questions. Once again, Charles stepped in.

"Jasper," he called. "Wait a moment. We can go together later this evening. We'll have to go there to return Miss Knight to the Daniels', and we can make the proper formal introductions then."

Jasper appeared not to hear him, or was in fact deliberately ignoring him, and continued to prepare to call on the former Brigadier. Charles didn't repeat himself. He knew when Jasper had his mind set on a plan, there was no reasoning with him. And honestly, he was happy to have one more evening without him. He felt a considerable amount of relief as his brother left and, with a lighter heart, he set about procuring some food for the three who remained.

Without the looming presence of his brother — for the time being — Charles was able to relax somewhat during the meal. That Miss Knight had been introduced to the worst of Jasper's behaviour and had not run screaming was a good sign. Though she *had* asked rather nervously if Jasper was always like that.

"Jasper tends to be a grumpy person," Beatrice had commented flatly.

Charles watched Miss Knight wriggle in her seat and, for the rest of the meal, he waited for the question.

"I hate to be indelicate," she began quietly, after they'd finished dessert.

Here it comes, Charles thought sadly.

"But I have heard things — rumours — that your brother rather drinks to excess. Is it true?"

"Would it matter to you if he did?" Charles replied, feeling disappointed.

"Of course not, I just —" Miss Knight began.

This caught Charles so off-guard that before he knew he'd done it, he had risen from the table and was steps away from embracing her. The two ladies looked at him strangely when he stopped in mid-stride, Miss Knight having abandoned the latter half of her sentence.

"Yes . . . I . . . Well . . ." *Very articulate, Charles.* He cleared his throat awkwardly. "It's just . . . I think Mr Daniels will be expecting you back soon."

Why did he say that? He didn't want her to leave, and from

the way her face dropped, she didn't want to leave, either.

Charles turned to Beatrice for help, but his sister only looked at him as though he'd said the most stupid thing in his life.

Miss Knight rose from the table, smoothing down the front of her dress. She avoided looking Charles in the eye. "Yes, you're quite right. Thank you for a wonderful day. I hope we can do it again." She started to leave, and Charles was feeling too guilty to stop her. Luckily, Beatrice had her wits about her.

"You can't walk!" she cried. "Don't be ridiculous. Charles will drive you."

Thank you, God, for smart sisters.

"Yes," Charles answered quickly. "We'll have to take the curricle. Jasper has the carriage."

The guilt washed away from Charles as Miss Knight lit up at the prospect.

"Oh, yes!" she answered. "If it's not too much trouble."

Charles couldn't help but laugh at her attempt at polite refusal and offered her his arm.

The evening was beautiful. Cold but not unpleasant, the cloudless sky revealed shining stars, watching them like thousands of curious eyes. The two of them were quiet for most of the journey, but there was an energy between them that crackled deafeningly. Charles chose to focus on the driving, but he was aware Miss Knight was watching him intently. He could feel his surprise for her in his coat pocket, as though it was burning a hole through the wool.

On entering St James' Square, they found Major Hartley's carriage still there, though, as it happened, he was just leaving. They crossed paths at the entrance to the square, though his brother merely nodded to them by way of acknowledgement.

Charles walked Miss Knight to the door. She stopped before knocking to be let in.

"Thank you for such a lovely day," she said quietly, playing with the fringe on her sleeve.

Charles took her hand and pressed a kiss against it. "It has been a wonderful day," he agreed. He paused for a moment, reaching inside his coat. He wrapped his hand around the small object within. He nearly lost his bravery and didn't bring it out. He took a deep breath.

"I . . . It may seem silly," he began, his eyes steadily focussed on his boot. "But I have something for you. Something to remember our day." His felt heat creep up his face as he opened his hands to reveal a stem of lilac, the same lilac that had been growing in the ruins at Witches' Cove. He had plucked one when Beatrice kept Miss Knight occupied.

Miss Knight stared at the flower and remained silent. Charles felt the wind being knocked out of him. He withdrew his hand quickly.

"It's only a silly token. I thought — But if you don't like it, I can get rid of it." Disappointment weighed heavily in his chest, and he struggled to speak without his voice breaking.

Miss Knight quickly reached out for his hand. "No. Please. I love it. I'm sorry. It's such a kind gift I didn't know what to say. I've never been given such anything so thoughtful," she explained in a rush.

Charles watched her dainty hands open his thick fingers to reveal the flower. Even though they both wore gloves, Charles' skin tingled ferociously. Miss Knight took the lilac from his hand and lifted it to her face, taking in the scent before holding it to her chest.

"I will see you again soon?" she asked quietly. "It doesn't matter to me what your brother does. I like you and Miss Hartley very, very much."

Charles barely heard her, consumed by a burning desire to reach down and kiss her. Somehow he restrained himself and had to be content with pressing another kiss to her gloved hand. "Absolutely," he promised. He gave her a low bow and bade her goodnight before returning to his curricle and driving away.

Annabelle stood alone in the doorway.

Her heart was beating so loudly she wondered if she even needed to knock on the door to let Mr Terry know she was back.

She was clutching the flower as she mounted the stairs to let her guardians know she'd arrived home safely.

"How was it, dear?" her uncle asked with great interest. He laughed warmly when all she was able to respond with was "wonderful," in a breathless and day-dreamy voice.

"I'll expect a full report in the morning," he joked as she kissed him goodnight and went up to her room. She climbed into bed, leaving the lilac pressed between two books so that she might preserve it.

As she fell asleep, her dreams were filled with burning cottages and ruins, lilacs, and Mr Hartley's blushing face.

CHAPTER SIX

"It was so beautiful, Uncle. It was just the *best* day."

"I'm glad you enjoyed yourself," Mr Daniels responded with a smile.

Annabelle had been happily giving her uncle an account of her trip with the Hartleys, hardly stopping to take a breath, let alone eat any breakfast.

Annabelle was sure she couldn't eat. Her stomach was still twisted and excitedly tight from Mr Hartley's generous gift the night before. She tried to convince herself it wasn't such a big thing, but she couldn't help herself. His gesture *had* to mean something.

Men don't just give flowers to any old companion, she had thought to herself over and over throughout the course of the night.

"Surely it couldn't have been the *best* day?" Mrs Daniels piped up when Mr Daniels had risen to fetch more coffee. "What about our trips with the Evanses?"

It transpired that not long after the party had left for Witches' Cove the day before, the Evanses had arrived, announcing they wanted to make a trip that day. They were disappointed and most angry to learn that Annabelle wasn't at home, particularly Mr Evans.

They had spun Mrs Daniels a story that Annabelle had most definitely agreed to take a trip with *them* that day. The woman was annoyed and mortified by her niece's behaviour, apologising profusely, and she'd been berating Annabelle all morning.

"Gregory is such a nice man, dear. *And* he's in the army. Very respectable."

Annabelle cast a look of despair at her uncle as he sat back down at the table.

"Now then," Mr Daniels cut off his wife. "That's enough of that. I think we all understand what you think of Mr Evans' virtues." He gave Annabelle a sly grin and addressed her. "I have some news that might interest you. Last night I received a visit from Major Hartley, brother of your Mr Hartley."

Annabelle cringed. "Uncle! He is certainly not *my* Mr Hartley," she cried, though she very much wished he was.

Mr Daniels waved his hand and continued. "Regardless, his brother called on me yesterday evening. He's an interesting fellow, though I do think I prefer the younger brother." He winked at his niece. "He came because of my time in the service with his father in Bombay. He expressed a wish to know more about his father's time there, and to be acquainted with those who knew him. We chatted for most of the evening, and I discovered that the Hartleys grew up not very far from the estate your aunt and I've inherited. He says he knows the area well, and I thought it might be nice if we invited the family to come with us when we inspect it in a few weeks. Having a *local* guide would be infinitely helpful."

Annabelle's eyes lit up, and her heart was doing a very good impression of a drum roll.

"That is *quite* out of the question," Mrs Daniels exclaimed wildly from the other side of the breakfast table. Annabelle's face fell.

"To what do you object, my love?" Mr Daniels asked calmly.

"I can't think of leaving Bath now," the woman replied indignantly. "Why I've only just reconnected with Mrs Evans — it'd be rude to leave. We don't have to be at Godshollow straight away."

"My dear, Mrs Evans will be here next year. And, now you've reconnected, you'll be able to re-establish a decent correspondence," Mr Daniels countered with all the serenity that Annabelle was lacking in that moment. "But of course, if you wish, you may stay here with her, and Annabelle and I will journey to Godshollow."

"What if Annabelle doesn't want to go?" the old woman asked indignantly, not giving up. She cast Annabelle a look as if to suggest she wasn't allowed to want to go. Annabelle thought her aunt looked as though she was having a spasm.

"Annabelle?" her uncle addressed her with the confidence of a man who already knew the answer. "Would you like to see Godshollow or stay here in Bath?"

Annabelle hardly waited for him to finish the sentence before answering. "Oh, Godshollow, yes. More than anything!"

"That settles it," he announced, satisfied.

Mrs Daniels huffed and flustered in her seat. "Well, then, we surely must invite the Evanses to come with us as well," she argued. Annabelle looked to her uncle, panic rising up in her once again.

"I'm sure the Evanses have their own plans for the season, my dear. And we agreed we wouldn't let too many people know about the property before we decided what to do with it. It would be beneficial to have the Hartleys along, as they know the area so well. But I shouldn't like to advertise it much more than that," he tried to explain to his wife. Eventually she grew quiet, although she attempted to argue a few more times before giving up.

The conversation was ended, and Annabelle was in great spirits, though she was beginning to think the Fates didn't want her to be happy.

Not long after letters had been sent to inform the relevant parties about Annabelle and the Daniels' leaving Bath, the Evanses called to petition them to stay.

Carys wasted no time trying to make Annabelle feel guilty. "Are we not your *friends*? *We've* known you longer, are *we* not more deserving of loyalty?" she demanded.

Annabelle was sure Carys didn't care what Annabelle did. Her anger stemmed more from the idea that she saw it as an insult to herself.

"I wouldn't mind at all," the Carys continued. "Except that we haven't been invited too. It's the utmost insult, as our mother is your aunt's friend. They've been the closest companions these past thirty years. That must count for something." She nodded resolutely.

Annabelle tried hard to find the right thing to say. "I don't think anyone meant to insult you," she said carefully. "I'm sure if your mother spoke with my aunt and uncle . . ." She trailed off. She didn't want to be horrible, but she would rather the Evanses *weren't* with them at Godshollow.

"Oh, I wouldn't want to go if I had to ask." Carys sniffed. "No. *They* must ask *me* . . . us." She corrected herself at the last minute, though her words revealed her true feelings. "Where are you even going anyway?"

True to his word, Mr Daniels had not allowed his wife to explain to her friend exactly where they were going.

"Gloucestershire, I think," Annabelle replied quietly.

As expected, Carys' nose crinkled in disgust. "A dreary county," she remarked snidely. "We shall have infinitely more fun in Bath, I have no doubt. But if you'd rather be with the Hartleys than with us . . . well, it's your loss."

Gwen, who was more genuinely sad about Annabelle's departure, handled the situation much better.

"If you really are to go, then we must make the most of our remaining time together. Unless," she added cryptically, "anything should happen to change your mind." Her eyes seemed mischievous and her voice held an odd tone. Annabelle was suspicious, but she promised they would spend as much time together as they wanted.

Not long after they'd secured her promise, the two girls were called away by Mrs Evans and Mrs Daniels, who between them couldn't offer a good explanation as to why the twins were actually needed.

Annabelle was left alone in the drawing room. She'd just made the decision to leave and find the others when the door opened, revealing Gregory Evans. He strode in, bold as brass, and sat in the seat opposite Annabelle.

"Mr Evans." She dipped her head in greeting. He sat still, staring at her for a moment. "I don't know where the others have gone," she added nervously, trying to fill the awkward silence. "But I'm sure they'll return soon."

Mr Evans shook his head. "It's not them I wish to speak to," he said finally. He took a deep breath, clearly preparing for something. "Annabelle," he said at length. "Now I don't usually go in for English girls, and I certainly avoid friends of the twins, but you're not too bad."

Annabelle supposed he thought he was paying her a compliment.

"My aunt is also *kind* enough to *constantly* remind me that I'm of marrying age," he continued. He paused for a moment, clearly considering his words, which Annabelle thought must have been an incredible first for him. "I think it would be for the best if we were to marry," he said matter-of-factly, as if he were proposing a business venture as opposed to marriage. He looked at her expectantly.

Annabelle was completely shocked. "Mr Evans, I–I don't really know what to say! I wasn't expecting anything like this," she finally managed to answer.

"Come now. There's no need to be modest, *cariad*," he replied with cocky self-assurance, putting a hand on her knee. "I have it on good authority you're infatuated with me." A smug look decorated his face.

Annabelle couldn't believe what she was hearing. Her stomach sank, and she was thankful she hadn't eaten at breakfast. She moved his hand aside firmly.

"Mr Evans." She began her answer cautiously. "I don't wish to offend you or to be rude, and I don't know who your *authority* is, but . . ." She hesitated. She certainly didn't like him, but she didn't want to hurt him. She steeled herself and continued. "I don't know who your source is, but they're sadly misinformed. Mr Evans, you are a nice man" — she still felt a need to be polite — "But I never imagined you had *matrimonial* designs on me. And I have to confess that I have none on you. What we have is a friendship, nothing more."

"Oh please," the Welshman scoffed, visibly irritated. "You've been giving me every encouragement from the beginning!"

Annabelle was beginning to get upset. The idea of marrying this man was the worst thing she could think of.

"Mr Evans, it was never my intention to do any such thing," she exclaimed. She'd given up on trying to spare his feelings. "I may have done it inadvertently. If I have, I apologise, but I never did so on purpose."

Mr Evans was clearly angry now. He stood from his chair and began to pace. "So, what are you saying?" he demanded harshly, his voice loud and intimidating. "Are you turning me down?" His voice was laced with incredulity, as if she was throwing away her weight in gold.

Annabelle was scared but she forced herself to hold her head high as she answered as boldly as she could, "Yes, I am, Mr Evans, I cannot marry you."

Evans was becoming more and more irate and refused to accept Annabelle's rejection. "You English strumpet!" he yelled, his rage bouncing off the walls, striking Annabelle harder than any physical blow. "How dare you refuse me? What better do you think you're going to do? You're a foolish young chit and you're throwing away the best thing you're *ever* going to have!"

Annabelle couldn't help but shrink back in her chair as he paced.

"I cannot believe," he roared, spitting all over her, "that you've strung me along all this time and now refuse to have me. How *dare* you!" He moved to within inches of Annabelle's face, his whole body shaking with rage. For a brief moment, Annabelle was terrified he was going to hit her. Instead, he brought his face close to hers. "I'll make sure," he seethed, "that everyone in Bath will know what a lying, scheming trollop you are. Including your *precious* Hartleys."

Annabelle let out a gasp. Evans laughed viciously in reply.

"Is that what it is?" he accused. "You were hoping he might have feelings for you? Is it because he has more money than me? How shallow. But after this, he'll never want to go anywhere near you again. I'll make sure of it. Although" — he laughed bitterly — "it would serve you right to end up with a family like that. I hope you can hold your drink."

He finished his speech and left the room, nearly taking the door off its hinges as he threw it open in his wake. He ran straight into Mr Daniels.

Annabelle called out her uncle's name helplessly — thinking Evans was leaving, she'd allowed herself to cry.

"Is everything all right?" her uncle asked, rushing to his niece's side.

"No, it isn't," Evans fumed, his face straining with rage. "You said I could have her," he charged, pointing a menacing finger.

Mr Daniels calmly faced him, drawing himself up to his full height. He wasn't much taller than Evans, but he still bore the military air of his youth which made him a formidable figure. "I said you could marry her," he began, his voice level and measured, "*if*, and only if, she consented. Did you consent my dear?" He addressed Annabelle.

"No, Uncle. I didn't," she stated firmly, though she was still shaking.

Mr Daniels kissed the top of her head and hugged her close before turning back to Mr Evans. "Then you may not marry her, *sir*."

Evans' face was red with anger. Annabelle could practically see the rage fill his body. The Welshman attempted to argue, but Mr Daniels stared him down. Eventually, he slunk away and Annabelle could hear him angrily tell Mrs Evans and the twins that they were leaving. Annabelle thought she heard pottery break as they left.

Mrs Daniels soon came around the corner, looking flustered. "What is this I hear that you've rejected Mr Evans?" Her tone was stern. She wasn't angry, but she wasn't happy. Mostly disbelieving.

Annabelle looked to her uncle, who smiled and encouraged her. "I couldn't marry him, aunt," she explained. "I don't love him."

Mrs Daniels scoffed. "You stupid girl! You could have learnt to. It's naïve to think you can marry purely for affection. Young lady, it's time you pulled yourself out of those silly books and realised you aren't a heroine in a novel but, instead, live in the real world."

With that final, devastating jab, Mrs Daniels turned and ran after her friend.

Annabelle finally let her tears fall unimpeded. "I've been so foolish," she wailed morosely. "I've disappointed everyone."

Mr Daniels put an arm around her. "You made the right decision, my dear," he reassured. "The only reason I gave him permission to ask in the first place was my assuredness that you would say no." He sighed deeply and wrapped Annabelle into a tight hug. "I just thought he deserved taking down a peg — let him hear the word *no* for once in his life. I'm sorry he was so awful to you."

Annabelle gazed up at her uncle, tears clouding her vision. "He *is* very obnoxious," she sniffled. When her uncle laughed, Annabelle began to cheer up.

"I think I'm going to lie down," she suggested. She was completely drained. Were her uncle not holding her, she was sure she would have fallen.

Mr Daniels helped her to her room and gave her a gentle kiss on the forehead, reiterating his belief that she'd made the right decision.

Annabelle fell asleep nearly as soon as her head hit the pillow.

CHAPTER SEVEN

The next day, Annabelle was besieged by letters from Carys, Gwen, and Mrs Evans, accompanied by impassioned pleas from Mrs Daniels, all begging her to reconsider Mr Evans. The man himself, apparently, wouldn't lower himself to plead for a wife.

They all tried separately, using various methods, but Annabelle stayed firm.

We would be related. I'd be your cousin! Gwen suggested.

It would make him so happy. I've never seen him like this about a woman, was his aunt's attempt.

Well. It's not like you could do much better. What makes you think our family isn't good enough? asked Carys, completely unaware of the irony of her lecturing Annabelle about the situation.

"We've been good to you, haven't we?" Mrs Daniels argued when she cornered Annabelle at breakfast. "It would make everyone so happy, and I know your parents would be contented to see you married. I *owe* this to Mrs Evans. She's been a very dear friend to me. Won't you do this one small thing for me? After everything I and your uncle have done for you?"

The constant bombardment was making Annabelle miserable, and she was found by Mr Daniels in the late afternoon, locked in his study, crying her eyes out.

"They all hate me," she wept, throwing herself at her uncle. "But I just can't do it. I *can't* marry him. I can't love him, I barely like him. I know the family means a lot to Aunt Moira, but he will never make me happy, and I am certain I will never make him happy either."

Mr Daniels hugged her and tried to calm her down, but she was feeling absolutely wretched.

"Aunt Moira will make you disown me, I'm sure!"

"That won't happen," Mr Daniels replied strongly. "I do think you made the right decision, sweetheart, I do. And I'm sure your parents would agree."

"I know what will cheer you up," he said after a long period of silence. "Why don't we visit the Hartleys and finalise our plans?"

Annabelle stopped crying and sniffled in a very unladylike manner. "But Mr Evans promised to tell them what an awful person I am. They'll never want to come with us now."

Mr Daniels sighed tiredly. "I'm sure that the Hartleys are too smart to believe anything that man says. But I also suspect they are ignorant of the event. I received a note not ten minutes ago asking me to bring my papers for Godshollow."

Convinced by his words, Annabelle was overjoyed at the prospect of meeting with people who wouldn't harass her about Mr Evans, and she eagerly looked forward to an afternoon of not having to discuss the affair at all.

She rushed upstairs, well aware that her appearance must be quite shocking. She pulled out a small vanity mirror and began to get ready.

She washed her face with cold water, trying to rid herself of the red puffiness that surrounded her eyes. Then she brushed her hair and tied it up, having cared little about it that morning when she woke. Finally, she put on her nicest day dress.

As she regarded her appearance in the mirror, she began to laugh hysterically as she thought of what an absurd event her wedding with Mr Evans would have been. She had no doubt Carys would have spent the whole day making nasty remarks about her dress and telling all who would listen that Annabelle was a second choice.

She didn't realise just how long she'd spent laughing over it until her uncle came looking for her.

"Please, darling, don't cry anymore."

"I'm not crying," Annabelle sputtered out between heaving breaths. "I can't believe he really thought I would marry him. He's never said more than five words to me that were not about himself. He is rude and mean. And he doesn't even read novels, Uncle! How can I marry a man who has never read Fanny Sparrow and never intends to?"

Her uncle patted her kindly on the shoulder. "At least you've cheered up," he told her. "Now, come along, every second spent here is a second less with the Hartleys."

The pair left St James' Square — Mrs Daniels was still moaning, complaining, and wailing about Annabelle's selfish behaviour and had elected to stay at home.

They reached Green Park within the half hour, taking their time to enjoy the day. In contrast to Annabelle's previous mood, the weather was bright and clear, even as the sun was beginning to set.

Mr Daniels knocked on the door of the Hartley residence and announced himself and Annabelle to the doorman, who opened it and showed them in.

Major Hartley was in his study, and Miss Hartley was in the drawing room. Mr Hartley was running errands in the town but would be back shortly. Annabelle tried not to be disappointed.

Mr Daniels went to speak with the Major while Miss Hartley invited Annabelle to sit with her and take tea.

"I have the newest instalment of *The Amatory Adventures of Arturo Avalon*. Have you read it yet?"

"No, I haven't, I've been a bit . . . busy." She felt as though Miss Hartley was certainly somebody she could talk to about her problems, but she didn't want to think about it. "Tell me everything," she implored, working up excitement for the new story.

"Well, Arturo Avalon has completed his quest to find the Sacred Chalice of Immortal Wisdom, yes. That was where we left him. Now he is journeying back to Camelot with his love, the fair maiden Auriel, when suddenly he has to defend them both from a pack of ravenous wolves that have been bewitched by the evil sorceress Romanaugh, who wanted the Chalice for herself so she might defeat the Grand Witch of Goodness.

"How wonderfully terrible!"

The girls spent the afternoon reading and rereading the excerpt and speculating over what would happen in the next instalment.

"There's no way he can get out of this one!" Annabelle asserted.

"But they can't kill the main character," Miss Hartley countered.

"Wait. Wasn't he given that magical flute a few instalments ago?"

"Of course! He can soothe the cursed beasts!"

"Far too easy." Both girls turned to see Mr Hartley watching them from the doorway.

"That's nowhere near heroic enough for the incredible Arturo." He stood in a ponderous pose for a few seconds.

Annabelle's mouth went dry seeing him casually lean against the frame, his slender legs crossed, his hair ruffled from the outside wind.

"I know how they get out of it," Mr Hartley announced, a devilish grin on his face. Devilish, because he proceeded to stand there in silence, not telling them of his theory.

"Well, do tell us then. How do they escape?" Miss Hartley laughed, rising to his bait.

"Yes, please do," Annabelle added, eagerly leaning forward in her chair.

Charles smirked. "You were having such fun coming up with ideas, I don't want to spoil it for you. You see, my idea is so ingenious there can be no other explanation, and it'll just make you sad you hadn't thought of it yourselves," he teased.

His sister promptly threw a bundle of lace at him from her nearby work box. "You're infuriating," she cried, exasperated. "You try." She turned to Annabelle. "He seems to like *you*, he might actually listen."

Annabelle laughed and put on her most charming and persuading air. "Dear Mr Hartley," she began, sickly sweet and overly exaggerated, trying to contain an escaping giggle. "Please would you do us the great honour of sharing with us your theory on the escape of Arturo Avalon? It would give us the greatest pleasure to hear it. We promise we won't be jealous. In fact, no doubt we will bow to your superior intellect and masterful storytelling skills. You do tell stories so well." She finished with a flutter of her eyelashes. She hoped she wasn't being too absurd, but she had a safe feeling neither of them would be mean if she was.

Miss Hartley couldn't contain her laughter. "Bravo! What a wonderful petition indeed. You'll have a hard time refusing that, my dear brother."

"Quite," the man agreed. Then he smirked again. "You know, since it was Miss Knight who so eloquently petitioned me, perhaps it's only her I should tell. I'll come and whisper it in your ear, madam, if I may." He knelt beside Annabelle and she knew her face was overset with a deep blush as he pretended to whisper confidentially in her ear. Her insides twisted deliciously as his breath blew across her skin.

"Mr Hartley," she stuttered slightly. "Surely you wouldn't be so cruel." She barely maintained her composure with him so close.

Mr Hartley sighed dramatically. "You're right," he conceded. "It's just not within me." He stood and sought out an available chair. "Gather round," he proclaimed, like a teacher with a group of students. "And I shall tell you how Sir Avalon truly escaped this peril."

Charles took great joy in creating the most absurd story he could. It had taken his mind a few moments to recover from being so close to Miss Knight, but something about her was off. She didn't seem quite as bubbly and enchanting as usual. Charles made it his mission to cheer her up.

" . . .and that is how they shall escape."

"With a pineapple?" Beatrice asked sceptically.

"It's a wonderful idea," Charles countered. "It's so ridiculous it must be true. Is that not so, Miss Knight?"

As the afternoon turned to evening, and the evening turned to night, Charles was happy to see Miss Knight in much greater spirits. And he was bitterly disappointed when Mr Daniels came in to tell Annabelle it was time to go home. He wasn't ready for that yet.

"Actually, sir," he petitioned, on the spur of the moment. "I was wondering if you would lend us your amiable niece for the evening. We have some wonderful stories to tell her, and we'd love to talk about what we can do at Godshollow."

"I think I can allow that," the old man replied happily. "Annabelle, I'll see you later, my dear. Do behave," he teased with a wink.

"She always does," Beatrice assured him. Then she went to inform Jasper of their additional dining company.

Charles was left with Miss Knight, and where she'd been excited a moment ago, she now looked worried and was fretting with her dress. She was pulling at it and flattening it, all whilst looking as though she might bolt out of the door at any moment. No doubt she was worried that her appearance wasn't enough for Jasper. He hadn't given a very good impression of himself to her.

Charles decided he had to step in. He walked over to her and gently removed her hands from her dress. "Miss Knight," he said firmly. "You look beautiful, please stop worrying. It won't matter to Jasper how you look." That was a small lie, but he hated the idea that anyone could make her feel as though she wasn't beautiful.

Once again, Charles found himself far too close to her, and far too tempted to kiss her. She was looking up at him with those beautiful eyes that communicated to him her most private feelings.

He leant closer to her, tilting his head slightly, his eyes fixed on her lips. His skin grew hotter and tighter as he watched her little pink tongue dart out to wet the tempting red of her lips.

"Mr Hartley . . ." she whispered quietly, her hands coming up to rest on his arms.

Charles felt as though he was going crazy and the only thing that could cure him was her kiss. His head swam and his pulse beat wildly.

"Dinner!"

Charles jumped backwards, nearly tripping over the nearby footstool.

Miss Knight just watched him with wide eyes. He could tell she'd been expecting him to kiss her, too. Charles cursed himself inwardly.

He was playing a dangerous game. This couldn't continue. He was being unforgivably selfish, and the longer it went on, the more he and Miss Knight stood the chance of getting hurt badly. But he couldn't resist her. He was sure that going to Godshollow was a bad idea.

After his stern talk with himself, Charles took a breath and tried to push down his feelings.

"I'll escort you to the dining room," he said to Miss Knight, trying to keep his voice even. A jolt went through his body when she happily took his arm, this delicate touch even more intimate than her being in his arms a moment ago.

You love her like a sister. You love her like a sister, he repeated in his mind. She can never be anything else.

When they joined Jasper and Beatrice in the dining room, Jasper cast an appraising eye over Annabelle's dress but didn't say anything. Charles shot him a sharp look to make sure he didn't.

That's something you'd do for a sister, he tried to convince himself.

As with most meals involving Jasper, this one began awkwardly. Charles sat opposite Miss Knight, but he could feel her anxiety from across the table. He wanted to reach across and comfort her, and now more than ever he was annoyed by his brother's behaviour. He might have even preferred if Jasper was drunk instead of this holier-than-thou social posturing he was doing now.

Next to him, Beatrice looked as awkward as he felt. "It's such a great kindness that the Daniels and Miss Knight have invited us to Godshollow," she babbled. It was a nervous habit of hers to talk too much. "It would've been a shame to lose such a great companion if you had left me here alone," she lamented to Miss Knight.

"I see!" Charles cried in mock indignation next to her, trying to lighten the atmosphere. "I'm not good enough company, is that it?"

"That's exactly so," Beatrice replied jovially, sticking her tongue out at her brother.

Charles contorted his features to display mock hurt and turned to Miss Knight. "My dear Miss Knight, you think I'm good company, don't you?" he asked.

You tease Beatrice about it, it's a perfectly valid question, his mind told him.

But you don't care nearly as much about Beatrice's thinking you good company or not, the devil's advocate in his conscience countered.

"I think you're most excellent company, Mr Hartley," Miss Knight answered sincerely, putting a big smile on Charles' face.

"I think," boomed Jasper's voice from the head of the table, "that you're all being childish."

His brother's interruption effectively ended the conversation for a while. Charles sighed internally and sadly watched as Miss Knight nervously pushed the food around on her plate. She looked so pretty when she was smiling, he was determined to see that smile again.

A man can wish a sister to be happy.

"Do you know much about Godshollow, Miss Knight?" he asked in an attempt to break the tension that had developed.

Miss Knight shook her head sheepishly. "I must admit I don't," she replied timidly.

"Well—" Charles began. But he was soon cut off by his brother.

"I'm surprised, Miss Knight. I assumed you would have done your research, asked around, sent enquiry letters and the like." Charles and Beatrice both rolled their eyes at each other and sent apologetic smiles to Miss Knight. "Oh well," their brother continued, "I shall just have to tell you."

"Actually, Jasper, I was about to—"

"Godshollow was built just before the Civil War, in the 1640s."

Charles sighed deeply. He'd wanted to tell Miss Knight the story so she would look at him again as she had when he was recalling the tale of Witches' Cove or inventing fanciful adventures for Mr Avalon.

Jasper wouldn't add the gothic details that would delight

her, that would take hold of her imagination and make her eyes light up.

You're sure you think of her as just a sister? his conscience piped up again.

At the head of the table, Jasper positioned himself into his most superior pose — the man liked when he knew more than other people — and continued his narrative.

"It was built as the home of a nobleman who'd left Court and sought a peaceful life. He built it far from civilisation so he wouldn't be disturbed. Not a bad idea in my opinion." Jasper sniffed superciliously. "When the war broke out, Godshollow became a royalist stronghold. Because of its placement deep in the forest, at the edge of a cliff, it went undiscovered by Cromwell's men for most of the war.

"In the last year of the war, it was laid siege to. The inhabitants were captured and the castle left abandoned, seized from the royalists as punishment. It remained unoccupied for many years, almost falling into disrepair until it was gifted to the family of Mr Gordon, who bequeathed it to your uncle in the 1690s." He paused.

Miss Hartley glanced at Charles with worry.

"The property could have belonged to my relatives," Jasper began heatedly.

Here comes the drama.

"Had Gordon not duped my great-great-grandfather out of it."

There it is.

Jasper left no doubt about his bitterness over the matter, and Charles found it absurd that he thought it reasonable to complain to the niece of the man who had inherited the property. What was he expecting Miss Knight to do? Throw herself at his feet and beg for forgiveness? Promise to get her uncle to transfer the title as soon as possible? Charles resisted the temptation to laugh at his brother, and out of the corner of his eye he saw Beatrice pinch the bridge of her nose. But Jasper hadn't finished.

"As it happens," the elder man remarked childishly, "Great-Great-Grandfather Stephen went on to build something much better a few miles away. It's since been torn down, but it was much grander than Godshollow has ever been."

Miss Knight looked helplessly at Charles, and he was only able to shrug his shoulders at her. This brought forth a small musical giggle from the beautiful girl.

Then her eyes widened, and Charles could guess what she was thinking of.

"Wait. My uncle owns a castle?" she asked in wonder.

He couldn't help but laugh. "I told you she'd say that," he teased Beatrice.

Charles watched as Miss Knight's face briefly morphed into an expression of embarrassment, then it quickly changed back to the bright, cheery, enough-to-knock-Charles-from-his-seat smile.

"Oh my," she said excitedly. "There must be stories about a place like that?"

"Naturally." Charles smiled, mirth curling his lips. Then he caught Jasper scowling from the end of the table. "But perhaps that is a story for another day. We have to have something to talk about on the long journey there."

Miss Knight frowned gently but nodded her head in agreement once she'd sneaked a look at the eldest Hartley.

"Though," Charles added, unable to bear her feeling an unhappy emotion. "I can say that my rectory is very near to Godshollow. It's in a quaint little village in Falton Bay. Perhaps we could take a trip there?" His heart beat rapidly at the hopeful expression with which Miss Knight regarded him.

It's perfectly reasonable for a man to want to show off his home, he argued with himself futilely.

"I certainly won't have the time," Jasper interrupted. "I will be far too busy to show you around the area, you understand. Brigadier Daniels and I will have much to discuss."

"I'm sure Beatrice and I will be able to do a satisfactory job in your place. We know the area just as well as you do," Charles answered rather irritably. He hadn't really had any intention of Jasper joining them in their adventures.

Miss Knight was much more tactful. "Thank you for your kindness, truly," she began. "I understand. And while it's regrettable, I don't wish to get in the way or be a nuisance to Mr Daniels. He'll have a lot of business to attend to. I'm sure you'll be a great help to him."

She was a smart woman—she'd realised the best way to deal with Jasper was to flatter his ego.

"I am very looking forward to this trip," she added, and Charles didn't know if he was seeing things that weren't there, but he was sure she'd looked at him with a special smile as she spoke.

Once the dinner was finished, Charles would have been quite happy to have Miss Knight with them for the rest of the evening, but clearly Jasper had had enough of *entertaining* visitors. No sooner had the dessert plates been taken away, Jasper promptly told Miss Knight he would escort her home.

She gave Charles and Beatrice a sad little wave, clearly not wanting to leave, but dutifully followed Jasper out of the building.

When they were alone, Beatrice turned to Charles with an evil grin that made him feel very nervous.

"You're in deep, aren't you?" she asked teasingly.

"I don't know what you mean," Charles responded noncommittally, indicating he didn't want to talk about the matter. But Beatrice was determined.

"You weren't exactly inconspicuous when you were mooning over Miss Knight at dinner," she teased, giving him a playful tap.

"I was not," Charles asserted, though deep down, he was worried he'd embarrassed himself.

"Don't worry." Beatrice laughed. "I don't imagine Miss Knight would be offended at the idea. She was practically the same over you."

"Really?" Charles tried to keep his voice as disinterested as possible, but his stomach was a twisted mass of nerves.

Beatrice looked at him with smug satisfaction. "Oh yes," she assured him. "She looked at you more than she did at her food."

"You're being ridiculous," Charles told her. He hoped that was true — the idea that Miss Knight might care for him excited him greatly — but Beatrice's suggestion was absurd. She had to be teasing him.

Beatrice shrugged her shoulders. "Well, believe what you want. I'm going to bed." She gave Charles a kiss on the cheek, but she couldn't resist one last parting barb. "Have fun dreaming of Miss Knight."

Despite all his mental assertions that he thought of Miss Knight as just a sister, he knew deep down his sister was right, and the young lady did indeed fill his dreams when he was asleep.

CHAPTER EIGHT

When she returned from the Hartley's lodgings, Annabelle's uncle sat her down.

"So, my dear. I have agreed with Major Hartley that we shall leave for Godshollow on Friday next."

"So late?" Annabelle couldn't help but ask. She really didn't want to stay in Bath anymore.

"It's only a week, darling," her uncle soothed, but Annabelle was far from convinced.

"Must we stay?" The idea of being in Bath for much longer filled Annabelle with dread. She had to focus intently to keep her breathing normal.

Mr Daniels patted her shoulder kindly. "That's the other thing I want to talk to you about." Annabelle tilted her head questioningly. "Your aunt has decided she's going to stay in Bath when we leave. She'd going to lodge with Mrs Evans. I was going to ask whether you wanted to stay with her, but I think I already know the answer."

Annabelle giggled, gently nodding.

But she felt conflicted. With the way her aunt had been about the proposal, Annabelle was glad she wouldn't be with them. But, of course, such thoughts made her feel guilty.

She was also worried that without Mr Daniel's sobering influence, her aunt might run away with her perceived slight of Annabelle refusing Gregory and Mrs Evans would wholeheartedly encourage her.

"I want to come to Godshollow with you," Annabelle answered resolutely, albeit unnecessarily.

"Of course. I shall be glad of your company. And I suspect our guests will be too."

Annabelle felt happier now she had a definite leaving date. The only problem was that between now and then there was going to be a ball, and Mrs Daniels was adamant that Annabelle should attend. She had tried to refuse, saying she didn't have any nice dresses left, she would just sour her aunt's mood, and even tried to claim illness, but her aunt was unmovable.

Annabelle was worried sick about the gossip the Evanses would be able to disseminate before the ball. Mr Evan's threat hung heavy in her mind.

Everyone in Bath will know what a lying, scheming trollop you are.

"I think it's only fair," her aunt complained, when Annabelle broached the subject once more the day before it was to happen. "You have already disappointed me," she accused. "I will not allow this behaviour."

Mr Daniels had tried to step in, but his wife was annoyingly stubborn, and he knew there would be no disagreeing with her. It seemed easier to concede on this point than have a full-blown argument that would result in the dredging up of every issue she'd ever had in her life.

So, on Wednesday night, two days before leaving for Godshollow, Annabelle found herself in a carriage, wearing her nicest dress, her body threatening to ruin it by making her sick. Her aunt had applied far too much rouge to her face, failing to understand that Annabelle's paleness had nothing to do with her natural complexion and everything to do with the severe anxiety that clung like black tar to her soul. She was feeling positively wretched, and she was certain the ball would offer no distraction.

As she alighted from the carriage, she took a deep breath, trying to centre herself. Perhaps this wouldn't be as bad as she feared. She tried to remember how this sort of thing went in her novels. She thought about *Miss Scarlet's Scandal* and *Whisperings in Willowswood* and tried to emulate those heroines, being bold and fearless, content in the knowledge they'd done nothing wrong. She pushed her shoulders back and held her head high, but truthfully, she didn't feel brave at all.

"Annabelle, you can't spend the evening in the carriage," Mrs Daniels snapped.

Slowly, Annabelle followed her aunt into the ballroom, and immediately her worst fears were realised. The second she stepped inside, she felt nearly every eye in the room turn to her, and within moments the disparaging glances and hushed whispers began. She tried to be as inconspicuous as possible, but her efforts were in vain. Partygoers grew quiet as she neared them, and some purposely avoided her. She felt as though the whole room was turning from her.

Mrs Daniels was at her side, but naturally she didn't notice, too consumed in her usual hunt for the Evanses, and they were soon separated. Annabelle was left on her own in a sea of unfamiliar faces, many of whom did not look on her favourably. She tried her best to blend into the upholstery.

Nobody was brave enough to speak to her directly about the rumours they'd heard, but she overheard enough to know what she was accused of.

"*I* heard she flirted with him, led him on, all but promised herself to him before turning down his proposal," one person said to another.

"Yes. I hear he was interested in his cousin, but Miss Knight caught his attention, promised him *everything,* and now the cousin will not have him because of the slight against her," another agreed.

"Even worse, she was Miss Evans' *friend*! She must have known her feelings."

"I think she was luring in Evans until the Hartleys arrived.

Once she saw how much richer Hartley was, she dropped Evans like a plagued rat."

"I'll tell you what. *I* heard the Hartleys have been invited to holiday with her and her chaperones. I bet she'll be setting her cap at the eldest Hartley now."

"She's a devious, cunning, social climber is what she is!"

"The only just thing would be if no man wants her at all after this."

It took all of Annabelle's strength not to dissolve into tears in the middle of the room. Her chest grew tight, her breathing quickened, and her eyes started to blur, stinging tears which she forced not to fall.

Whenever she heard Evans' name, anger ignited in her body, and she began to shake. She wanted to scream at them all that they were being unfair and petty by gossiping, but she knew that would do no good.

Light-headed and weak, Annabelle was finally broken when the Hartleys entered the ballroom and they were treated with the same silent contempt. She lost her resolve completely and ran from the room, managing to exit without crying but only by the smallest of margins.

Annabelle threw herself into a secluded alcove and sobbed furiously. Her head ached and her heart hurt. She was all alone. Her life was ruined. She'd been foolish to think she could ever be like the heroines she admired so much. She was young and foolish, and she had destroyed everything.

After five minutes of this solitude, Annabelle was joined by Miss Hartley.

"My dear Miss Knight, whatever is the cause of all this crying?" she asked gently, embracing the young girl, who was heaving and shaking with the ferocity of her sobbing.

"It's awful," Annabelle sobbed. "Your brother will think so ill of me . . . They're lying, I swear . . . But no one will believe me . . . And they're being so rude about him . . . It's all so horrible."

"What is, dear?" Miss Hartley asked.

"I can't believe he would lie like this." Annabelle sniffled. "I'm not worth all this fuss. He can find himself another wife."

"Charles?" Miss Hartley asked in a bewildered tone.

"Mr Evans," Annabelle sobbed, barely able to breathe.

Annabelle felt Miss Hartley stiffen around her. "What has he done?"

Between tears, Annabelle told her the whole sorry affair, from her rejecting Mr Evans' proposal, to his vowing to reveal her *true nature* and now the people of Bath spreading the rumours.

"You poor thing," Miss Hartley soothed, "no wonder you're so upset. All that whispering and gossiping. It's just because they are bored *silk-stockings* with nothing to do. They're lazy busybodies."

"But they're saying such horrible things and implying Mr Hartley has played a part. I'm afraid this will hurt his reputation beyond belief and he'll never want to see me again," Annabelle disclosed. "Miss Hartley, I even fear that you will not want to talk to me after tonight."

Miss Hartley wrapped her arms around Annabelle. "First of all," she began in a calm voice. "I think we can dispense with formalities. From now on call me Beatrice." Annabelle nodded against the woman's shoulder.

"Secondly," she continued gently, "don't worry about Charles. Our family's reputation has survived much worse, and I know he's smart enough to distinguish fact from fiction. He cares about you and knows your character better than any who would spread these rumours. You're a beloved friend, Annabelle, to Charles *and* to me, and it would take much worse than this for us to abandon you."

When she finished, Annabelle relaxed slightly.

"And don't think this will deter us from visiting

Godshollow with you," the older girl teased.

Annabelle gave her a teary smile, before becoming down-cast again. "What of the Major?" she asked despondently. "I'm already beneath your friendship with my social status. After this, he'll never want you to speak to me. He'll never wish to associate with my family again."

Beatrice shook her head. "Our brother is in no position to be judging anyone by their reputation. You needn't worry about *that*," she said sternly. "Besides, it's quite possible this won't reach him at all. These people are simply looking for something to liven up their dull lives, I'm sure this will all be forgotten as soon as something new happens to capture the gossips' attention—which in Bath, could be in a few hours. Please don't be worried. We'll be gone soon, and they'll find something else to talk about."

"Really?" Annabelle sniffled.

Beatrice nodded. "Of course. Now"—she paused for a moment—"I don't think you're in a fit state to go back in there. So it's lucky I have brought some entertainment." Reaching into her reticule, the older girl pulled out a pack of cards. "Gentlemen do hate women playing with them." She laughed mockingly. "They're no fun to play with anyway."

The cards were dealt, and Annabelle and Beatrice played hand after hand, Annabelle's mood improving with each round of *vingt-un*.

That was until Mr Daniels came around the corner rather abruptly. He was straightening his cravat, and he had a gen-erally flustered air.

"Annabelle, my dear, there you are. I rather think it's time we were leaving," he suggested. She noticed he had her coat draped over his arm. "I don't think we are completely wel-come anymore."

Annabelle looked up, tears in her eyes, her face devastated. "Oh Uncle, I'm sorry. It's all my fault!" she cried, flinging herself into his arms.

"It's not your fault, my dear," her uncle promised kindly. "A young man of Mr Evans' acquaintance wouldn't keep his mouth shut and said something he shouldn't have. I simply let him know that I disagreed with him." His voice held a somewhat mischievous tone. "I don't know why they're making such a fuss. It's only a bloody nose. He'll recover, and it's no less than he deserved. Nevertheless, I think it best if we were to depart."

Annabelle nodded and turned to her friend, feeling lucky she could still call her so. "Thank you, Miss Hartley." She squeezed her friend's hand. "You've been so kind, I'm sorry to have kept you away from the party."

Beatrice smiled kindly at her. "It was no trouble. And don't forget, it's Beatrice now. I think Charles and I might leave as well, as all the good company are going home." She winked at Annabelle.

Annabelle chuckled and bid Beatrice goodbye as she linked arms with Mr Daniels. They left the party amid more whispering, but Annabelle held her posture stronger than before, and couldn't help but giggle at her uncle's handiwork when they passed a young man in the corner clutching a red-splotched handkerchief to his nose.

When Charles finally tracked his sister down, Beatrice was standing in the corridor, grim determination in her features.

"There you are," he exclaimed. "You left me on my own. I've been fielding snide remarks all evening. Do you have any idea what's going on?"

Beatrice took him aside. "We need to talk," she said sternly then told him all she had learnt from Miss Knight.

Charles felt sick.

"He can't treat her that way," he shouted indignantly,

uncaring of who heard him. "I'm going to tell him exactly where to go with that kind of behaviour."

"Please don't, Charles," Beatrice said softly. "It might make *you* feel better, but think how devastated poor Annabelle will be. She has a gentle, fragile heart. She would hate to think you'd been affected by this and she would never forgive herself if he hurt you. We should just go home."

Charles nodded slowly at the sage advice.

"I suppose so," he conceded. "It would be a bad example if a vicar were to engage in fisticuffs."

"Quite so," Beatrice agreed, linking her brother's arm. "We will just support Annabelle in whatever way she needs."

"Yes, we will have to show her the most wonderful time in Gloucestershire."

The pair re-entered the ballroom, and Charles felt his blood boil when he caught eyes with Evans, who just gave him a smug, satisfied grin. Then the cad swaggered over to them.

"Have fun with your harlot," the Welshman goaded, laughing. "You deserve each other, really — a gold-digger and a rich family with no fortune left. Ha!"

Charles knew Evans was trying to get a reaction from him, he shouldn't give in, but he had an overwhelming desire to slap that smug grin off Evans' face.

Beatrice tugged his arm sharply. "Leave him," she commanded firmly. "He'll taste justice. There's no need to lower yourself to his level."

Afraid if he opened his mouth, he would start yelling, Charles set his jaw and nodded brusquely, allowing his sister to lead him away.

"We'll see, love," Evans called to them as they walked off. "I'm getting all the justice I need."

Charles turned, absolutely ready to beat the man soundly, but instead he watched in shock as Beatrice marched up to the Welshman, pulled back her hand as if to slap him, then promptly stamped as hard as she could on his foot, taking advantage of his preoccupation with guarding his face. The room went deadly silent and Evans stood dumbfounded as Beatrice marched back to Charles and they left the ballroom.

"What was that about not making a scene?" Charles whispered through gritted teeth.

Beatrice looked at him guiltily. "He deserved it," she replied resolutely. "And I said *you* shouldn't make a scene. I didn't say I couldn't."

As Charles helped Beatrice into the carriage, she turned to him seriously.

"I think," she said gravely, "that it may be time for you to talk to Jasper about Annabelle. I don't want either of you getting hurt."

"But he will never agree," Charles countered. He felt like a despicable coward.

Beatrice sighed gently. "I'll leave it to your discretion, but the longer this goes on, the worse it will get."

Charles knew his sister was right, and he had to admit that he'd felt sick at the thought of Miss Knight being married to someone else — the idea that Evans had proposed to her made his stomach lurch. But what could he do?

He spent all night thinking about Annabelle, but by morning, he was no closer to figuring anything out and was utterly exhausted.

Chapter Nine

When Annabelle first came to Bath, she was sure she would find it hard to leave. Now she was preparing to go, and she couldn't have been happier to be leaving the city behind. In fact, she was certain she would never want to come back at all. She'd learnt a hard lesson about the nature of people, and she decided she didn't like the kind of people who lived in Bath.

Friday came, and Annabelle happily brought her luggage down into the square, eagerly awaiting her departure.

The Hartleys called at half-past eight o'clock, ready to lead the way.

Whilst the cases were being loaded onto the carriage, Beatrice took the opportunity to invite Annabelle to ride with herself and Charles. Annabelle gladly accepted, with her uncle's approval, and sat herself opposite Beatrice in the carriage. She waved to a disgruntled looking Mrs Daniels who was preparing to stay with the Evanses.

Mr Daniels settled himself in Major Hartley's carriage. They had decided that he would leave the carriage for Mrs Daniels' use, that she might join them later.

"Are you ready, ladies?" Mr Hartley called to his passengers.

"Yes!" they cried in happy unison.

As the carriages rolled out of Bath, Annabelle let out a deep breath.

"How are you?" Beatrice asked with sincerity and a friendly grasp of Annabelle's hand.

"Better for leaving Bath," Annabelle replied honestly. She could feel her worries fall away the farther they got from Bath and the vicious gossips. She breathed deep and rested back against her seat, watching the countryside roll past, the wind gently washing over them in the open-top carriage "I feel like Juliette from *The Bashful Miss Banbury*," she told Beatrice. "And like her, I will rise above those manipulative, scheming people."

"A wonderful attitude, Miss Banbury," Beatrice replied with a smile.

When they'd been travelling for a few hours, Mr Hartley called back to them from the driver's seat. "Mr Daniels suggested before we left this would be a good place for a break in our journey. Is that agreeable?"

The girls consented and the travelling party pulled into a nearby inn.

They all alighted, glad of the chance to stretch their legs.

"Let's take an hour, then we should get back to it," Mr Daniels suggested. "We can have some food, take a rest, and then complete the journey."

Major Hartley approved the idea, not realising nobody was asking for his permission. Annabelle laughed as the man looked taken aback when no one answered him.

Mr Hartley was being extremely kind to Annabelle. Even kinder than before, which Annabelle had thought would be a physical impossibility. She was certain he and Miss Hartley — no, Beatrice — had discussed the events of the ball, and she felt as though Mr Hartley was being overly nice to her, trying to show her he wasn't bothered by scandal.

Annabelle had to admit she was enjoying the extra attention, but she didn't want him to feel obligated to be nice to her. It rather wounded her ego to think he was only being kind to her because he had to.

Annabelle, you're being ridiculous. He was nice to you before that, silly girl. She proceeded to have a long argument with herself about whether or not Mr Hartley really, truly, honestly liked her. Her inner conflict was exacerbated when Beatrice suggested she sit on the driving bench with Mr Hartley.

"You'd be able to see Godshollow from a great vantage," the man himself had suggested.

Annabelle then spent the rest of the journey intensely aware of her proximity to him. She tried to make polite conversation, but she couldn't stop thinking about how close he was. Her body hummed with energy, vibrating the air around her. Mr Hartley had to keep his focus on the road, but on the odd occasion he did look at Annabelle, his gaze burned through her soul.

Every so often, their hands would brush against each other as she pointed to something or he moved the reins. At one point, Annabelle thought she might faint when Mr Hartley had to brake suddenly and held her close to stop her from falling off. With his strong arms around her, she found thinking coherently very difficult.

After hours of travelling, Mr Hartley slowed the horses' pace. "Close your eyes," he instructed Annabelle.

After casting him an odd look, she complied. She felt the carriage come to a stop and suddenly Mr Hartley's hands were over her eyes.

"I had to make sure you're not peeking," he whispered in her ear, sending delicious tingles down her spine. Then he moved her slightly, positioning her before he removed his hands.

"Open," he commanded. Annabelle didn't need to see him to know he was smiling — it was in his voice

She obeyed and opened her eyes, her breath drawn from her body as she gazed upon the sight.

They were on one side of a valley that sloped quickly downwards, going on so far that the trees looked like tiny wooden toys. Across the other side, resting at the edge of a rocky cliff, was Godshollow — the only sign that there was any human interference in the beautiful, ancient landscape — its high grey stone walls an eye-catching contrast to the surrounding evergreens.

"It's beautiful," Annabelle whispered reverently. She leaned back slowly. Mr Hartley's hands were on her shoulders, as he'd not completely removed them when he uncovered her eyes. As Annabelle let herself fall back, she was very soon pressed against his chest.

The moment was perfect. After everything she'd been through in the past week, she finally had one instance of utter bliss.

"Why have we stopped?" Beatrice asked, sticking her head out of the window. Annabelle saw the moment that Beatrice regretted her actions, the realisation dawning in her mind before she quickly apologised and disappeared inside the carriage.

Annabelle sighed deeply as Mr Hartley let go of her shoulders and took hold of the reins again. But her disappointment didn't last long.

As they drew closer, Godshollow only became more impressive. Annabelle couldn't find the words to adequately describe the phenomenal structure, and she was all at once awed and terrified. But most of all, she was excited. Thrilled, she was eager to see if the beauty of the outside was matched within.

As she surveyed Godshollow, she found it hard to believe her uncle now owned all of this. The building was amazing, bigger than anything she'd ever seen — it seemed absurd that all of this should be for just two people.

As they followed the disorienting, winding pathway up to the property, Annabelle could completely understand how such a large estate had stayed hidden for so long.

"I hope I never have to make this trip alone. I'm sure I'd never find the way," she commented.

Mr Hartley chuckled beside her. "I'm sure it will be easier the more you do it. As it is, I'm glad we have Jasper's guidance."

Finally, they emerged from the dense forest into the copse within which sat the behemoth stone structure of Godshollow. Tingles shocked the length of Annabelle's body as she took in the grandeur of the architecture that loomed over her. She felt a great sense of history radiating from the building, as well as a sense of mysterious promise. She'd never felt so connected to a building before and couldn't wait to explore it.

She, Beatrice, and Charles were the last of the party to arrive, thanks to their brief stop to take in the scenery. The Major had gone ahead with Mr Daniels, and they were currently giving instructions to a young boy about the horses. Given the swiftness of events, from the death of Mr Gordon to the possession of the building by the Daniels, most of the staff were still in residence at Godshollow and were hoping to be able to remain there.

Annabelle maintained a stunned silence, her mind working hard to try and comprehend the majesty she was seeing.

Lost in her thoughts, she squealed as she was taken by surprise and lifted into the air. She clung to Mr Hartley — who had done the lifting — in shock and gripped the front of his coat, even after he'd set her on the ground again, her eyes squeezed shut.

"Annabelle, I think you can let him go now dear." Mr Daniels chortled as he approached them.

She felt Mr Hartley laugh as he placed his hands on hers to gently ease them from his collar. She blushed and apologised profusely, though she was finding it quite hard to think, being so close to him. "I'm sorry," she stammered.

"It's quite all right," the gentleman assured her. "I did ask if you needed help dismounting. I thought you'd heard me. I didn't want you falling and hurting yourself." He gave her a quick wink before moving around the carriage to have a word with the stable boy.

Annabelle could barely breathe. Her heart was racing, and she couldn't move. She was hardly aware of her surroundings until her uncle called for her.

"Come along in, Annabelle, dear."

She was the only one left in the courtyard. Whilst she had been recovering from her brush against Mr Hartley, the eldest of that family had begun organising.

"We should eat," the Major announced in a loud voice. Being the member of their group who knew the area best, he'd appointed himself as leader and had taken it upon himself to make all executive decisions, not that he'd told the others. "And then we should take a quick look around and allocate rooms. We can do a thorough tour in the morning." He didn't wait for anyone to reply before turning and going into the house.

"You heard him, troops. We have our orders," Mr Hartley joked before offering his arm to Annabelle. "Mr Daniels, if you'd be so kind as to accompany my sister, I'll follow you with Miss Knight."

Mr Daniels made a grand flourish of bowing and offered his arm in a most dramatic fashion, producing a delighted giggle from Beatrice and an embarrassed groan from Annabelle.

As Mr Hartley led her across the threshold into the atrium, Annabelle came to a stop and gasped loudly. She'd never been inside a home as grand as this in her eighteen years, and it was far beyond anything she'd imagined. She was awestruck.

Mr Hartley stopped beside her. "Were you expecting it to be dark and musty, everything covered in ominous white sheets?" he teased.

"Well, it would have been very gothic," Annabelle replied cheekily. "But this is amazing! It's so bright and colourful. That has to be the most beautiful painted window I have ever seen."

"Yes. That was installed by the late Master Gordon," said a voice. Annabelle was so surprised that she let out a small shriek.

"Sorry, Miss. I didn't mean to scare you." A man emerged from a side door and held his hand out to Mr Hartley. "Brigadier Daniels, sir?" he asked, clearly sceptical that a man so young would be a brigadier.

"That would be me," Mr Daniels interceded, emerging through the front door. "Though it hasn't been brigadier for longer than I would care to say." He shook the man's hand warmly.

"Sir. I'm Mr Peters, the steward. I'm the one you've been communicating with through your letters."

He began a long, involved speech about his duties in the house and the work he'd done in preparation for their arrival, and how happy the staff was to have a master again whilst getting to stay in the home they loved. Honestly, Annabelle hardly took in a word, too busy regarding the house with wonder.

"I'd be quite happy to give you a tour of the grounds, sir," the steward said excitedly. "I also have a list of all the furniture and possessions you've been left by our previous master. You will have seen a copy of the will, I assume, detailing what you have inherited. We can go through it, if you like."

Mr Daniels patted him on the shoulder. "First and foremost, I think right now what we need is some refreshment."

"Of course, of course, sir. Right away. We've prepared food for you, cold meats and such. We didn't know when you were arriving, so we didn't do anything hot or the like, in case it'd spoil. While you eat, we'll bring your luggage in. We've pre-pared rooms for you all. Patrick" — he snapped his fingers at the boy who'd been tending the horses — "start bringing the cases in." He turned back to the newly arrived party. If you would follow me, sirs, madams."

Peters led them across the foyer towards a lavish double staircase. As she stepped onto it, Annabelle saw images of the glamorous Isabella Sheppard from *Isabella Imprisoned* de-scending the staircase for her first ball in her lavish, opulent gown, drawing the attention of all who saw her when she was announced.

"Oh!" she cried happily as they went farther into the house. "This is magnificent. Can you imagine what it must have like when it was first built? All those balls, the ladies in those large, beautiful dresses! It's almost sad, isn't it?"

"Why sad?" Mr Hartley asked at her side.

"Just to think of the life they'd had. How the war must have ruined everything." She sighed contemplatively. "I've been so focussed on this place being like my novels, I forgot that real people lived here. That sounds so silly doesn't it?"

She looked up at Mr Hartley, but his expression was un-readable. He was silent for far too long, and Annabelle feared she'd offended him.

"I think," he said, slowly drawing out Annabelle's agonis-ing, "that we would all much rather live in a world of novels. There's nothing wrong with not wanting to think about pain and suffering. Unfortunately, we all have to face it at some time."

Annabelle couldn't discern at all the emotion of his tone. He sounded wistful, resentful, nostalgic, frightened and a whole host of other contradictory feelings.

The group were shown into a large dining room.

"This isn't the grandest dining room, though," Peters said with pride. "I thought I'd save that for tomorrow."

But Annabelle thought this room was astounding. It was tall and wide, with enough space to comfortably seat a family of twenty.

The walls were a deep red, with flower patterned paper covering the bottom half. Two large windows gave the room more than enough light, which counteracted the minimising effect of the oak furniture that lined the room.

A vast dining table was the main decoration, and it sat in the middle of the room, groaning under the weight of plates upon plates of food, everything required to soothe the soul of a weary traveller.

"I would've preferred a hot meal." Major Hartley sniffed, regarding the feast with a contemptuous glance. "But this will do."

"It's perfect," Beatrice put in quickly, whilst Mr Hartley rolled his eyes.

They ate mostly in silence. None of them had realised just how hungry they were, and they were too busy eating to hold a conversation. The rest of the silence was accounted for by their general awe of the place. As everyone looked about them, they wondered how the rest of the house must appear if this was only the second-best dining room.

After they'd eaten and the plates were cleared away, Mr Peters returned to show them all to their rooms so they could settle in and unpack. The castle was a maze of hallways and rooms.

"Is there a map?" Annabelle asked the steward as he led them down yet more corridors, up more stairs, and through more doors. "I fear I won't be able to find breakfast tomorrow."

Mr Peters chuckled good-naturedly. "I'll send a servant to help you," he promised.

Annabelle thanked him profusely as she was shown to her room. She was staying in a large room at the end of a corridor in the East Wing of the building. It was decorated with blue paper and had almost as much space as the dining room. The best thing was that she wasn't far from Beatrice's room. She imagined it would be very easy to feel isolated in a house as big as this.

"What do you think of it all?" Beatrice asked as the two girls sat on her bed.

Annabelle gazed around the bedroom, trying to order her thoughts. "It's astonishing," she replied after a moment. "It's a lot to take in, it's all so beautiful. I've never seen anything like it! Wonderful!" She rose from her seat to look out of the arch window. "So wonderful."

"It is," Beatrice replied. "You know, my mother loved this place. Apparently, she used to visit quite often when she was a child."

Annabelle turned away from the window to face her friend. "You never told me that!"

"I just did." Beatrice laughed in reply.

"Well . . ." Annabelle couldn't think of a comeback. "You should have told me sooner," she weakly finished. She turned back to look out the window, gazing at the beautiful countryside spread before her. "How old were you when you left the area?"

"I was young, barely six, I think. I can't remember clearly," Beatrice said slowly. Annabelle sat down beside her. "Jasper was older, of course, and Charles must have been very small. When our mother died in childbirth, our father was devastated. He tried for a few years to continue living as we had been, but he found he couldn't face staying in a house with so many memories. He moved us to the secondary family home in Worcestershire. When he died, Jasper tried to move us back here, but our old house was too expensive, so we stayed where we were. I only have vague memories, but they're some of the happiest memories I have. Of course, Charles has his rectory at Falton Bay, which isn't too far from here, but it's not quite the same. It's nice to be back."

Annabelle gripped Beatrice's hand and offered her a handkerchief to dry her eyes. They sat in silence for a moment as Beatrice composed herself. Mr Hartley's head appeared around the door frame.

"Ladies," he greeted them with an over-the-top bow. "It would seem that the other gentlemen have settled for the evening in their pursuits, leaving us to our own devices. Luckily, before we left Bath, I made sure to pick up the latest Fanny Sparrow instalment. I thought perhaps we might have a reading in the drawing room, if that's agreeable to you." He smiled brightly, waving the booklet at them.

Annabelle was so excited about the prospect that she was on her feet before Mr Hartley had even finished his sentence. He held out his arm for her, and with Beatrice trailing behind, he led the girls to the aforementioned drawing room.

It was a cosy room with a few large chairs and a bookshelf that covered one whole wall. Being there felt to Annabelle like being enveloped in a warm hug.

Mr Hartley had clearly expected the girls to agree to his plan and had arranged for the fire to be drawn, which now steadily roared, adding to the atmosphere of the room.

Mr Hartley was very gracious and offered Annabelle the first choice of seats. She made herself comfortable on the half of the sofa closest to the fire and was delighted when Mr Hartley claimed the seat next to her. Beatrice selected the armchair.

Mr Hartley began to read, and Annabelle was captivated, both by the story and his voice.

They finally found out how Sir Arturo had escaped and, testament to Miss Sparrow's writing skills, her solution took them all by surprise.

Annabelle was disappointed to find they'd come to the

end. The story had left them in *such* an exciting place — Arturo and Auriel were in the middle of their wedding when the ceremony was interrupted by a cloaked figure who shouted that he had an objection.

Also, she'd rather enjoyed simply listening to Mr Hartley's voice. She was certain he must be a very good pastor. In all honesty, he could probably make reading a recipe for ink sound exciting.

After some pressing by Annabelle, and Beatrice as well, Mr Hartley conceded to read some more, and the three of them spent the evening reading their favourite Fanny Sparrow short stories. Eventually, they all agreed the hour was late and they were, in fact, quite tired.

When Annabelle finally slipped into bed, she stopped a moment to take a deep breath and allow herself to take in everything she'd experienced that day. Her mind raced with all that she'd seen, and once again, as she drifted to sleep, her dreams were eerily vivid.

She was running. It was night, but the moonlight lit her way as she ran down a large dual staircase, her dress billowing behind her. She didn't know who or what she was running from, but she soon found herself in a thick forest. She ran through the foliage, her dress catching and ripping, and all she knew was she couldn't stop. A nearby snarling of wolves spurred her on faster.

She continued to run until she reached the edge of a path leading to a hidden pool. She managed to stop herself before she fell.

She could hear soft speech, somebody reciting something into the night air. She recognised it as the poem that Arturo Avalon had used to break his fair Auriel from the hypnotic trance of Romanaugh.

Such beauty hast there never been,

In all of our long history.

Thou, maiden fair, art the only one mine eyes do see,

I worship thee most fervently.

Come to me and betwixt our souls,

Will be a holy union.

The voice was entrancing. Annabelle found herself drawn to it. She looked around the area of the pool for signs of who it was, and sure enough, she saw the clothes of an Arthurian Knight lying on the rocks at the edge of the water. He must be swimming.

She leant forward to try and get a glimpse of the man below, but he was just beyond her view. She pushed aside the brambles and branches to get a better look. Eager to find him, she moved too far and lost her footing. She slipped off the edge of the path and tumbled down the steep bank, landing finally with a sharp splash into the cold water.

Submerged in the black cold, she couldn't find her way to the surface. She became entangled in long, ensnaring weeds and tried to cry out, letting precious air escape in bubbles. She struggled and struggled until she felt strong arms wrap around her and pull her to the surface and the open air.

She clung to her saviour as he swam her to the shore, and his touch felt oddly familiar. He laid her on the bank and placed a hand to her chest to check if she was still breathing. His hand brought a bit of warmth against her skin, and she realised how cold she was.

She blinked the water from her eyes and looked up into the face of Charles Hartley!

The moonlight lit his face, streaked by the trees, and all the breath that Annabelle had regained was taken away by his beauty. He was so close she could see the myriad of colours that made up his hypnotic blue eyes. She felt as though she was drowning all over again.

They remained in that position for what felt like an eternity. She was very aware of her body pressed against his, particularly because his clothes lay on the rock near her head.

Finally she spoke, her voice a soft whisper. "Thank you for saving me."

Charles remained silent, gazing at her with a burning intensity. Water dripped from his obsidian hair, made even darker by the water. Big droplets rolled down his bare, muscular arms where they were placed either side of her head to hold himself up.

Eventually, he answered her, his voice low and hypnotic. "I couldn't deprive the world of such beauty," he purred, once again mirroring the words of Arturo.

Annabelle's heart pounded against her ribcage. "What can I do to repay you?" she whispered, squirming under his gaze, but trying to be confident. He leant his head forward until it was inches from her own.

"Kiss me," he suggested, his voice so quiet that Annabelle only just heard what he said.

She replied by bringing her hand to his face, closing the gap between their lips.

CHAPTER TEN

Annabelle was awakened by a knock on the door of her room. She pulled on her wrap and opened the door to Beatrice and a maid who'd come to see if she required any help getting ready for the day.

Annabelle gladly accepted. She wasn't used to having a maid to help her. She was accustomed to ready herself, requesting help from her sisters when desperate, but it was nice not to have to contort herself to secure her dress.

"How was your first night?" Beatrice asked excitedly. Annabelle was happy that being here made her friend so cheerful.

She considered the night she'd had. That wonderful dream. Her fingers rose without her consent to touch her lips, where she swore she could still feel that kiss.

She realised with a start she hadn't answered the question and Beatrice was regarding her oddly. "It was . . . fine," she replied, trying to sound nonchalant.

Beatrice pursed her lips shrewdly. "More than fine, I'd say, if one were to judge by the look on your face. Be assured you can tell me anything."

Annabelle observed her friend, trying to imagine how on earth she would explain her dream.

"I did it too," Beatrice confessed.

Her words threw Annabelle for a loop and she began to become flustered.

"I stayed up all night reading gothic novels as well!" the older girl finally announced.

117

Phew! Annabelle breathed a sigh of relief. She wanted nothing more than to talk to Beatrice about her dream — it was what one did with one's closest female friend. But given that the object of her dreams was her friend's brother, she decided that would be too awkward and too embarrassing to discuss.

"Yes," Annabelle admitted, like a school child who'd been caught cheating. "I couldn't help it."

"I know!" Beatrice replied animatedly. "This is the perfect place to read them. Why, as I read *The Ghoulish Temptation of Geraldine Taylor* I swear I could hear the ghostly wails of those trapped souls!"

Around ten o'clock, the ladies made their way down to the breakfast room.

Major Hartley and Mr Daniels, they were informed, had already breakfasted and had gone hunting for the day. Mr Hartley however, sat at the table, his face hidden behind a book.

"Which gothic horror do you have there, dear brother?" Beatrice tried to peek into the book in his hands.

Mr Hartley peered at them from over the top of the pages. "It's the accounts for Falton Bay," he explained with a slight grimace. "Far less exciting, but just as terrifying." He set the book on the table and rose to help the ladies into their seats.

"It's about time you showed up," he chided teasingly. "I'm starving, and I've been informed that it's polite to wait for company to arrive before eating. So I've been sat here all alone, only allowed to *look* at all this delicious food."

As Annabelle watched him speak, she couldn't draw her gaze from his lips. Would kissing him be as amazing as it was in her dream? She tried not to stare, and she prayed he didn't notice her fascination with his mouth, but she couldn't draw her focus away. Luckily, Mr Hartley was otherwise occupied.

Beatrice had sent a piece of bread flying through the air in the general area of her brother's head. Annabelle couldn't contain her laughter as the projectile caught him unawares, hitting just above one ear. Despite being surprised, he managed to catch it rather handily.

Mr Hartley gave a dramatic sigh and cast Beatrice a disparaging look before turning to Annabelle, waving the chunk of bread in an authoritative manner. "Don't encourage her, young lady," he threatened as they all tried to contain her laughter. It wasn't working, and poor Annabelle was struggling to breathe.

"Just look what you've done, Beatrice," he continued. "The poor girl can't breathe. Here, my dear, try some water."

Annabelle accepted the glass and managed to get her hysterics under control.

When everyone had calmed down, they discussed the plans for the day.

"We certainly must explore the castle more thoroughly," Beatrice stated. "A place like this must be full of secrets."

"You've been reading those novels again," Mr Hartley teased.

"This was once a military stronghold," Annabelle countered. "They must have had places to hide."

"Exactly." Beatrice stuck her tongue out at Mr Hartley.

"Naturally." The man gave another dramatic sigh. "That will be our morning's activity. But what shall we do at lunch?" Mr Hartley clearly had his own ideas, as he didn't wait for the girls to respond. "I was talking with Mr Peters, and he says there's a waterfall not far from here. I say we have ourselves an adventure."

Beatrice heartily agreed to the plan, but Annabelle wasn't able to respond. At the mention of a waterfall her mind had been flooded with the images of her dream. The shimmering moonlight, the hypnotic song, Mr Hartley's dazzling eyes. Overwhelmingly, she couldn't stop thinking of the man's state of undress and the kiss they'd shared at the water's edge.

"Miss Knight? *Miss Knight*!"

"Annabelle!"

Annabelle snapped from her reverie and found the Hartley siblings watching her with concern. How long had she been sitting there, not moving or speaking? Hopefully not too long.

"I think it's a wonderful idea," she said, trying to hide her flustered manner. "Perhaps we could even go for a swim!"

Because that's going to stop you thinking about him with no clothes on. She groaned quietly. Embarrassment assaulted her, threatening to pull her apart from the inside. "I'll go and ask if we can have a picnic lunch put together," she blurted out, rising quickly to her feet. She dashed from the room, and only once she was safely around the corner did she begin to slow. She took deep breaths, trying to calm herself.

Just think of something else. Anything *else!* Annabelle tried her hardest to distract her mind, but all roads led to Hartley.

When she arrived at the kitchen, she was able to focus on the picnic and received a brief respite. But once she re-joined her companions, her stomach began to buzz as though a swarm of angry bees dwelt therein just at the sight of Mr Hartley's smile.

"As you two have a much superior knowledge of the gothic," Mr Hartley hinted, "I shall trust you to point out any hidden passages or secret rooms. What do you think are our chances of leaning on a bookshelf and discovering a secret dungeon?"

Mr Hartley teased the girls for the whole exploration as they moved from room to room, visiting the kitchen, the servants' quarters, the bedrooms, the parlours, and dining rooms, asking them each time what fantastical things they hoped to find. But despite his joking, Annabelle knew he was enjoying it as much as they were.

Their exploration was significantly waylaid when they discovered an attic room in one of the abandoned towers.

"This is just like *Captured Miss Caroline*," Annabelle exclaimed blissfully, running her finger through the thick layer of dust gathered on a chest of drawers. She abandoned the dresser and went to examine the small, arched window. "Can't you just see Caroline looking down to see her hero, waving her handkerchief so he can locate her?"

"Miss Knight," Mr Hartley commented behind her. "Are you implying they've been keeping innocent young girls locked up in here? Because if you were . . . I'd be very worried if I were you." Annabelle could hear the teasing in his voice and turned just in time to see the man slide out of the room and pull the door shut behind him.

Annabelle looked at Beatrice, and the two girls started laughing. The older girl tried the doorknob, but they figured Mr Hartley must be holding it, as it wouldn't budge.

"Mr Hartley, you're a terrible tease," Annabelle accused through the wood, stomping her foot petulantly for effect.

"You're incorrigible," his sister chastised. "If you keep abusing her, Miss Knight will throw you out."

They heard Mr Hartley chuckle on the other side of the door.

"How will she do that if she's stuck in there?"

Beatrice gave Annabelle a mischievous wink. "Well then," she addressed Mr Hartley nonchalantly. "You'll just have to spend the rest of your visit with Jasper."

Annabelle had never seen a door open so fast. Both girls were overcome with a fit of hysterics at the utterly horrified look that adorned his face.

"I'll be good, I promise." He offered his arm to Miss Knight, but his sister took Annabelle's arm instead.

"Come, Miss Knight, let's leave this degenerate to himself." The girls left the room as they heard Mr Hartley running to catch up with them.

Charles was thoroughly enjoying this trip to Godshollow. Miss Knight's enthusiasm was infectious, and it was so freeing to be as positive as she was. Ever since their father had died, Charles and Beatrice had mostly existed in a state somewhere between sombre and serious. Having the freedom to enjoy themselves was rather exhilarating. "I think," he said, as his stomach growled at about a quarter past one, "we should begin our trek to our waterside picnic."

As he mentioned this, he noticed Miss Knight wore a peculiar expression She almost seemed embarrassed. But what on earth had she to be embarrassed about? Was she scared of water? Heights? Whatever it was, he would have it out of her — he had no wish for her to be uncomfortable.

"Is something worrying you, Miss Knight?" he asked.

He'd noticed over the last few days that Beatrice and Miss Knight had been using each other's Christian names. That made him remarkably jealous, but he was a gentleman — a clergyman at that — so he wouldn't take such a liberty until he was invited to do so. However, that hadn't stopped the name from falling from his lips when he was alone, usually after waking from a dream.

The young woman looked rather like a burglar caught midtheft at his question. She coughed self-consciously. "Nothing's the matter," she answered, though Charles was far from convinced.

As they followed the directions the maid had given them to get to the waterfall, traipsing through the wild beauty of the forest that surrounded Godshollow, he kept an eye on her. When they reached their destination, instead of being anxious or worried, she turned a shade of most startling scarlet.

Beyond confused, Charles decided that the young woman was simply remembering a scene from one of those novels she and Beatrice loved so much and that was causing the blush.

A deep desire ignited in him, and he desperately wanted to ask her what she was thinking of. His body felt as if set alight, to think of her describing the creative scenes Fanny Sparrow had concocted, to say out loud the things he'd only considered in dreams.

Charles remained quiet for most of their meal, choosing to sit back and observe. As it was, the deafening rush of the waterfall made conversation nigh on impossible, but his sister and Miss Knight gave it their best go.

"This is so much better than Bath!" Miss Knight attempted to shout over the noise.

"Indubitably! I much prefer standing under a flow of water than bathing in a tub," Beatrice responded in her own hoarse shout.

His sister's hilarious misunderstanding aside, Charles was certainly happy to be out of Bath. The farther from Mr Evans the better. He thought Miss Knight looked far happier now they were out of Bath. Her distress had been replaced with her usual enthusiasm and charming exuberance. She was so bright and bubbly it was hard not to be swept up in her emotions, and Charles was sure he was smiling now more than he ever had before in his life.

Whilst Miss Knight was looking at some manner of creature in the small pool, Charles' sister sidled up to him.

"You have to tell her how you feel," she prompted.

Charles wildly hushed her and checked to make sure Miss Knight had not overheard them.

Beatrice raised an eyebrow at him. "This is just childish," she chastised. "You clearly have feelings for her. She clearly has feelings for you. And *you* have clearly decided you will pay no heed to what Jasper thinks of the whole thing."

Charles looked down, scuffing the toe of one boot against the other. "It's not that simple," he replied lamely.

"It really *is* that simple," Beatrice countered impatiently.

"What's stopping you?"

Charles sighed and gazed at the beautiful girl kneeling at the water's edge. "Jasper, for one."

Beatrice huffed indignantly, obviously not accepting that.

"No, really," Charles continued. "I may think I'll be able to stand up to him when the time comes, but when have we ever been able to say no to him?" He gave his sister no chance to answer his rhetorical question before moving on to his next point. "Second, she doesn't want me. She wants one of the heroes from her novels. A dashing, brave, handsome, mysterious man, not a second-son vicar with a tiny house on the coast."

Beatrice regarded him carefully. "Well," she said at length. "I think both of those excuses are utter rubbish. I posit that you are just too scared. But this is something you have to decide for yourself. You're a grown man, and you certainly don't need me telling you what to do. I just want you to be happy. And I want her to be happy too."

There was warning in that last statement, but she left him to think over what she'd said, whilst she rejoined Miss Knight.

He certainly did have a lot to think about. By the time the group had returned to the grounds of Godshollow, toured the gardens, and joined Jasper and Mr Daniels for dinner, he had almost made up his mind to speak to his brother — in fact, he'd decided and re-decided about six times by then.

Unfortunately, his brother didn't seem to be in a good mood.

"I trust you all found *useful* employment today and managed not to annoy the servants *too* much," Jasper voiced as they entered the room. Charles knew there would be no talking to him today. He resignedly sat down on a nearby chair.

Miss Knight was happily regaling her uncle with that day's activities, and Charles could see his brother was of the disposition that he would rather be anywhere else.

"The gardens are marvellous, aren't they?" Mr Daniels was answering his niece.

"They are adequate." Jasper sniffed, clearly unimpressed. Then he turned to Mr Daniels. "Where's that girl with our brandy?"

Ah. Charles thought sadly. *Not that he's going to be any more amenable once he's had it.*

He decided to postpone his discussion with his brother until he had the bravery to face any of his brother's many tempers.

Miss Knight continued to detail their exploits to Mr Daniels, but after a little while, he put his hand up to stop her.

"I am sure you've had a wonderful day." He smiled somewhat conspiratorially. "But I have some news which may yet add greatly to your happiness."

Charles looked at his sister, then Miss Knight, then his brother. The former two seemed to be just as confused as he was, whilst the latter was clearly involved in more important things now that his drink had arrived.

Mr Daniels looked smugly at the three young people. "Major Hartley and I"—the other gentleman did not look up from his brandy glass—"struck upon a plan while in Bath. We thought it would be a splendid idea if we were to hold a ball here."

Though Mr Daniels had said *we,* implying that both of them had come up with this idea, Charles was sure his brother had very little to do with the actual decision.

"We wanted to assess the state of the place before we made any definite decisions," Mr Daniels continued. "But I think you'll agree that Mr Peters and his staff have kept the house in wonderful order. We approached him on the subject, and he assured us that Godshollow would be quite fit for our purposes."

"We sent the invitations this morning," his brother

announced, finally looking up from his drink. "It'll take place two weeks from tomorrow. I have no doubt some guests will be staying for a few days after the event as well. You" — he turned to address Charles, Beatrice, and Miss Knight — "will of course be required for the evening, but may do whatever you wish with the day. Though help in preparing for our visitors would be appreciated."

That was so typical of Jasper, asserting that he expected them to help in any case but trying to seem fair by giving them the *opportunity* to volunteer.

All three proclaimed they would love to help.

The rest of the evening continued rather much the same way as the last one. Mr Daniels and Jasper went off to discuss things ahead of the ball and Charles once again offered to read for the ladies. Whilst they said yes, they took considerably longer that the night before to join him in the drawing room.

When they did arrive, Miss Knight looked apprehensive. For one dreadful moment, Charles thought his sister had decided he was taking too long and had told Miss Knight of his feelings herself, but then he calmly reminded himself Beatrice wouldn't behave like that. At least, he hoped she wouldn't.

For the rest of the evening, his heart beat wildly against his chest, and when he retired to bed, he knew he would be unable to sleep.

CHAPTER ELEVEN

Annabelle woke early the next day. Once the maid helped her dress, she took advantage of the time to sit at her window and enjoy the view of the woods in the early morning light. The sun cast its rays through the sparse branches and into the clearing. Once again, she found herself wishing she could draw, so she might capture the image and preserve it.

Her mind began to wander. This time, she wasn't thinking of her novels but the history of Godshollow. "Oh, the things this castle must have seen!" She sighed nostalgically.

She tried to imagine hearing the roar of Oliver Cromwell's New Model Army of parliamentarians as they crashed through the forest. She heard the sounds of fighting — clashing steel, shouting men, musket balls, and arrows striking stone walls echoing all around her. She could see the figures force their way through the trees, surrounding the castle, leaving no way out.

She imagined herself as one of the women, fearfully watching as the men went to battle, listening at the door for sounds of the enemy.

A burly soldier would knock down the door, an evil smile twisting his thin lips.

She would scream loudly, throwing anything she could get her hands on to repulse the intruder. When that didn't work, she would scream again and do her best to scurry past the barbarian and escape.

That would be when Mr Hartley would enter. Hearing her

screams, he would come to her room, sword poised, ready to battle the renegade who dared harm her.

"Unhand her," he would cry, sending the blade of his sword flying through the air, catching the attacker on the arm.

Frightened by such a display of aggression, wound bleeding, Cromwell's man would run.

When they were alone, Mr Hartley would take Annabelle in his arms and kiss her passionately, and promise that he'd always love her, no matter what. "Annabelle," he'd say, "you are my – "

"Breakfast!"

She was snapped from the daydream. "Annabelle, you're missing breakfast." Beatrice stood in her doorway, hand on her hip, as though she was scolding a child.

"I am?" Annabelle replied, dazed. The thought worked its way through her mind for a moment. "I am!" she cried at length. She rose to her feet frantically as she heard Beatrice laugh. The older girl approached.

"Nobody's angry," Beatrice assured her. "We were just wondering why you hadn't come down."

"I'm sorry," Annabelle replied. "I was daydreaming." She felt a heat begin to work its way over her body.

"Oh! About anything nice?" Beatrice asked casually as she fastened the corset strings.

"Nothing in particular," Annabelle answered, glad she was turned away so Beatrice couldn't see the lie in her face. Nevertheless, Beatrice clicked her tongue knowingly.

"Well," she said casually. "There's lots to stir the imagination here. Come and join us when you're ready." Then Beatrice left the room, but not before beaming a very wicked smile at Annabelle.

Oh God! She knows I was thinking about Mr Hartley. But I can hardly talk to her about my fantasies of her brother!

Trying to calm her distress, Annabelle focussed thoroughly on getting dressed, taking each moment slowly, and being meticulous so her mind couldn't wander any more.

When she walked into the breakfast room, the others had finished eating and were deep in discussion about the ball.

Luckily, there was a little food left, and as she took her place at the table, Beatrice handed her a tart.

"Good morning, dear." Mr Daniels greeted her with a warm smile, though his conversation partner, Major Hartley, merely nodded in acknowledgement.

"Good morning, Miss Knight. I feared we'd lost you to the gothic delights of Godshollow," Mr Hartley teased with a smouldering look.

Annabelle laughed gently. "It's a distinct possibility," she riposted, tongue-in-cheek.

"Well then," Mr Hartley replied. "I'll have to keep a close eye on you. Nobody knows what sort of trouble you could get into in a place like this."

"There's always trouble wherever *you* go," Beatrice retorted with a smirk before Annabelle could form a response. The grin Mr Hartley had given her had set her insides fluttering, and she was fighting hard to maintain her lucidity.

"That's enough of that," Major Hartley boomed from the other end of the table, as though he were talking to a group of school children. "We need to sort out what jobs need doing for the ball. We haven't got time to dawdle." He pulled out a piece of paper and laid it on the table as Mr Daniels cast a look at the young people that let them know he found the Major's bossy attitude just as humorous as they did.

"So," Major Hartley announced importantly, not noticing the smirks of those surrounding him. "The Brigadier and I will make sure that the kitchen staff know what they are to do, and that they have enough food. Charles, you will talk with the stables and make sure there is adequate room for any guests, organise with Mr Peters about who will stay where when replies are received. And ladies" — he turned to Beatrice and Annabelle with an expression that left the latter feeling as though he considered women's work very unimportant—"you will make sure the house is presentable. Speak with Mr Peters and ensure that all is clean."

The Major then called their breakfast meeting to an end and made it clear he expected everyone to get on with their tasks immediately.

The next two weeks passed in a flurry of activity as preparations were made for the ball. There was a lot more work to be done than anyone had realised. Mr Peters had done a marvellous job of keeping the house together in the months it had been unoccupied, but the late Mr Gordon had only used a minimum of rooms.

That meant there were a lot of bedrooms to uncover, clean and make habitable, as well as sitting rooms and card rooms that hadn't been used in a very long time and would need to be aired out.

Annabelle didn't get a chance to see Mr Hartley much over the course of those weeks. They were both consumed by preparations during the day, and far too exhausted to socialise in the evenings.

All five of the Godshollow occupants ate together, but these meals too were busy, with everyone hungrily replenishing their energy or discussing the upcoming ball.

So, it wouldn't really be until after the ball that Annabelle would get to properly spend time with her friends.

On the day of the ball, after they had done all the last-minute touches to preparations, Beatrice asked Annabelle to visit her room.

"You can say no of course," the older girl said as Annabelle was let in. "I realise that it is out of fashion with the modern looks today, but I had to try."

She handed Annabelle a beautiful pale green dress detailed

with delicate white embroidery. The v-front dipped a little lower than anything Annabelle had ever worn before. But the moment she stepped into the garment, she felt stunning

"This is beautiful," Annabelle breathed as she stared at her reflection in the mirror.

Beatrice stood beside her with a bright smile, but teary eyes. "You look wonderful," she said gently. "This dress was once my mother's. It doesn't fit me, but I've always kept it, for sentimental reasons. I feel it needs to be worn for our first ball in this place that she loved so much, and it fits you almost perfectly."

Annabelle was overwhelmed and clutched her friend tightly. The only thing that kept her from crying was the generous labour Beatrice had put into her appearance.

When both girls had recovered from their intense rush of emotion, Annabelle returned the favour and helped Beatrice into a deep red, satin dress decorated with pearls and feathers.

Downstairs, they could hear some of the early guests arriving, but were informed by a passing maid that everything was under control. So the two girls indulged in their favourite shared pastime of reading Fanny Sparrow novels until Mr Daniels came to collect them for the ball.

Charles was standing in the corner of the hallway being introduced to a Colonel Phillips, the son of some late serviceman of his father's acquaintance, when his attention was captured by the arrival of his sister and Miss Knight. His breath caught in his throat. Miss Knight looked even more beautiful than he'd ever seen her—not only was her dress and her appearance dazzling, but her smile, and the way she held herself— as though this time she too knew she was beautiful—struck him dumb.

He was so entranced that he found himself neglecting his conversation with the Colonel. He ended the discussion rather abruptly and made his way over to the beautiful Miss Knight. At that moment, he wasn't aware of anything else other than her.

He wove through the crowd but when he reached her, he wasn't sure what to say. The words wouldn't come. After a few moments of awkward staring, he forced himself to speak.

"You . . . you look wonderful," he managed to say. Miss Knight began to blush, her gorgeously exposed skin turning almost the same shade as Beatrice's dress. He had a strong temptation to reach out and touch her, feel the warmth of her blush beneath his fingers. He restrained himself, but the yearning didn't subside, and he couldn't help but wonder if she'd feel the way he'd dreamt she did.

"Beatrice said the dress once belonged to your mother. I've never worn such pretty clothing," Annabelle said with a warm smile.

Charles felt a pang in his heart as he looked at his mother's gown.

Beatrice had always talked with Charles about their mother, but this was the first time he was presented with a possession of hers that wasn't an oil painting. Miss Hartley certainly didn't resemble the descriptions he'd heard of his mother, but nevertheless he found himself touched at the sight of the dress.

Tears began to well in the corners of his eyes, but he blinked them away. "Pretty isn't nearly adequate to describe how you look," he told her. He quickly tried to move the conversation to something else, when they were interrupted by a guest who was looking for more wine.

"You're General Hartley's son," the inebriated guest informed him, clapping him on the shoulder. "Come with me, I can tell you some stories." The man then looked at Miss

Knight. "Be a good girl and fill this." He thrust his glass into her hand.

Charles opened his mouth to tell this *gentleman* that Miss Knight wasn't a servant, but the young woman curtseyed politely and told them she would be back in a moment.

That was the last time Charles saw Miss Knight for at least half an hour, as she never returned with the drink. Whether she'd gotten waylaid or had simply decided not to get it, Charles didn't know. The man who'd interrupted them was drunkenly recalling his past exploits, little of which actually contained General Hartley.

As the man was about to launch into what Charles knew would be a long and rambling story involving travelling up the Khyber Pass, Charles rose to his feet abruptly.

"Excuse me," he said, not even bothering to think up a good excuse before he left the other man's company.

He scanned the room for any sight of the red hair that surrounded him in his dreams. At length he saw her. She was standing in a corner with a greying old man. She did *not* look comfortable. Charles made a beeline for them. As he drew near, he began to hear the man's conversation.

"My son has just made Lieutenant Colonel," the old man was bragging. "I wish I'd brought him tonight. You're just his type. He would have enjoyed meeting you." Ignoring Miss Knight's obvious discomfort, he reached out and stroked a lock of her hair. "Though, were I younger, you'd be my type as well, my dear."

Charles had drawn near to them by then. He laid a hand on the man's shoulder, ready to say something, but another voice was heard before he could speak.

"When *you* were younger," stated an old woman with a pointed nose and sharp eyes, who poked a walking stick in the man's direction, "your *type* was any young girl with ample bosom and ample fortune, as I remember it, Captain

Georges. And from what I hear, your son's even more roguish and rakish. Tell me, is he still courting that heiress in Chepstow? The one engaged to the duke?"

The man mumbled and huffed a response before moving away to talk to someone else, his tail firmly between his legs. Charles laughed to see him slinking so.

"That man really shouldn't be allowed out of the house without his wife," the old lady said when Charles and Miss Knight turned to her. "She's very good at controlling him."

"It seems *you* handled him quite well," Charles commented with a smile. He offered his hand to her. She accepted and shook it firmly. "Mr Charles Hartley," he offered in introduction.

"Mrs Angela Lutton," she replied brightly. "Or should I say, Mrs General George Lutton?"

Annabelle introduced herself and gave Mrs Lutton a curtsey. "Thank you for your help with that gentleman," she said gratefully.

"You're more than welcome, my dear. Though you, young man," — she poked her stick at Charles — "shouldn't be leaving your fiancée alone with such men around."

Miss Knight blushed, and Charles baulked.

"She's not — we're not — that is to say — we have no — she's — there isn't — " he fumbled.

Mrs Lutton laughed. "I see." She winked at the pair. "Perhaps I should be leaving you with these gentlemen and their eligible sons, my dear," she teased.

Charles stiffened, though he tried to appear nonchalant. He saw Miss Knight firmly shake her head

"I see, indeed," Mrs Lutton muttered to herself in amusement.

When the old woman went off in search of her husband, Charles was left alone with Miss Knight, and once again words failed him. The thought of her being his fiancée filled his entire body.

"She seemed . . . nice," Miss Knight said awkwardly.

Charles could do no more than nod back. "How funny she thought we were . . ." She let the end of the sentence hang in the air between them.

"Indeed," Charles agreed, trying to seem aloof.

They continued in their awkward silence, neither meeting the other's eye, until dinner was called.

Relieved at being able to put an end to this uncomfortable scene, Charles escorted Miss Knight into the dining room.

Miss Knight, Beatrice, and he had been put together, as Jasper had demanded the head table for the highest ranking men, as well as himself and the Brigadier, of course. Mr Daniels had tried to argue on their behalf, but the three of them had agreed to avoid a fight. As long as they were together, they didn't mind.

They were soon joined by Mrs Lutton, her husband in tow, waving her place-setting. "There seems to have been a mix-up with the seating." She promptly swapped her and Mr Lutton's cards for that of some lieutenant or other who had yet to arrive. "Much better," she said happily as she sat down.

Over the course of the dinner, everyone had enormous fun getting to know each other better.

"Hartley. Yes. I was a few years ahead of him, but we served together for a time," General Lutton remarked. "I'm sorry to hear of his passing."

Mrs Lutton smacked her husband on the arm. "George! For goodness sake, they don't want to talk about that. This is a dinner party. It's time for tales of the delightful, not the morose."

Mrs Lutton was also riotously funny company. Not only were her nose and her eyes sharp, but her wit was like a razor. She was very quick and very smart. She reduced Annabelle and Beatrice to fits of laughter on more than one occasion.

Because of her husband's rank, she belonged to the higher echelons of society, but she carried none of the pomp and pride that came with that and was a refreshing addition to the company assembled at Godshollow.

"Then she asked me who had prepared such excellent potatoes. She nearly fell out of her chair when I said *I* had!"

The dinner finished, the ladies and gentlemen retired to various rooms. Some went to play cards, others to sit and listen to music — Beatrice had generously offered to play piano. The Hartleys and Annabelle were the youngest in the room by a few decades, so there was no dancing. This, however, didn't escape the eagle-eyed Mrs Lutton, who piped up at the end of the next piece.

"Come, my dear, play us something lively. I see Mr Hartley and Miss Knight are just itching to dance. Just because we're all too old and doddery doesn't mean they can't enjoy themselves." She spoke with such authority that nobody dared argue. Beatrice laughed as she selected the right music.

Miss Knight had tried to protest, but Charles wasn't passing up this opportunity. He directed her into a small corner. Being only the two of them, they didn't need the regular amount of space. As they faced each other, the music started.

"How are you enjoying your first Godshollow party?" Charles asked her, pretending as though they had only just met for the first time.

"Very well, thank you," she replied sincerely. "It's absolutely wonderful. And you, sir?" She let out a musical little laugh.

Charles felt his knees go weak. "Quite marvellous," he replied with a cough. He waited a moment until the dance brought them closer together. "Though this is by far my favourite part of the evening."

And it was. Having Miss Knight to himself, Charles didn't

have a care for anything else that was going on around him.

"You mean to say," Miss Knight responded teasingly, "that this is better than poor Mr Benton's unfortunate accident with his food, which saw it end in the lap of Lady Chapelsworth?"

Charles laughed as he twirled her under his arm. "That was quite a show," he agreed mirthfully, "but I'm enjoying this for an altogether different reason."

They fell silent again as the music arrived at a particularly energetic part. Eventually, they were able to talk once more.

"You know," Charles began, raking his eyes over her form. "I may have to petition Beatrice to let you keep that dress. You look amazing in it."

Miss Knight thanked him kindly as a blush rose up her face once more. "I think I've received more compliments this evening than I've ever had in my entire life." She laughed.

"Criminal," Charles replied.

Miss Knight tilted her head in confusion Charles decided that just wouldn't do for this young woman to be underestimating her beauty because of foolish young men who hadn't complimented her when they had the chance.

"You're exceptionally beautiful. You should be under a siege of compliments every single moment."

He'd done it again. He'd trapped himself. He had been unable to stop his thoughts from manifesting as speech and now all he could think of was kissing her.

Miss Knight was gazing up at him from beneath her lashes. She was clearly uncomfortable with compliments, but the way she responded to his made Charles want to do nothing else all night but praise her.

Their odd little dance progressed and brought them closer still. Her hand was on his shoulder, her body inches from his.

"Miss Knight—"

And then suddenly Miss Knight wasn't in his arms anymore. She was on the floor, clutching at her ankle.

"I caught my foot in the dress," she lamented. "I'm so sorry."

Charles dropped down beside her. "Have you hurt yourself?" His hands hovered over hers.

"I think I hurt my ankle. But I'm sure I'll be fine."

"Can you stand?" He helped Miss Knight to her feet. The young woman winced slightly as she set her foot down. That was enough for Charles. He scooped her up into his arms and carried her towards the sofa.

"I'm fine. I can walk," Miss Knight protested. But Charles was quite happy with her where she was. Then he starkly realised the other guests must be looking at them.

"It seems needless to stress your ankle," he said quickly, looking about him. He gently placed Miss Knight down upon the seat and saw Mrs Lutton watching him shrewdly.

"I see," Charles heard the old woman repeat as he left the room.

Annabelle's insides twisted deliciously. She couldn't think straight. The pain in her ankle was minimal, but her heart was racing like a galloping horse. She'd been so close to Mr Hartley, and he had held her so delicately. She was going to faint, she was sure of it.

"What an interesting young man," Mrs Lutton, opposite Annabelle, commented as Mr Hartley was called over to a group at a table. "And you're not — is he engaged to another?"

Through the haze in her mind, Annabelle heard Beatrice reply.

"No, he isn't."

Annabelle couldn't entirely focus, but she thought she heard Beatrice say something about Charles being indecisive and never able to seize the moment.

The words swirled around in her brain, but Annabelle

couldn't make sense of them. All she could think of was Mr Hartley's hands on her ankle. The warmth of his fingers had seeped beneath her stocking and her skin tingled.

At first, she'd cursed herself for being so clumsy. Something had been about to happen, she was sure. She'd been so close to Mr Hartley, and he'd been looking at her with such an intense gaze. But she had to ruin the moment by tripping over her own dress.

As she'd crashed to the ground, she'd damned her bad luck. Then, when he carried her in his arms, she sent a prayer to God that she would always be so clumsy when he was around.

She felt light-headed as she lay back on the sofa, her heart pounding against her chest.

"Perhaps you should retire, Annabelle," Beatrice suggested, placing a hand on Annabelle's forehead and recalling the girl to her surroundings.

Mrs Lutton clucked in agreement. "I think she has had enough excitement for one day."

Annabelle apologised profusely but admitted she was fatigued. That was hardly the truth, but she wanted to think over the events alone.

"Yes," Mrs Lutton continued in a matronly tone. "Twisted ankles are just the worst. Though" — the old woman smiled mischievously — "you *were* very lucky to have a strong man to help you."

Annabelle was sure she saw Mrs Lutton wink at her as Beatrice helped her from the couch.

As she lay in bed, Annabelle felt as though her whole body was throbbing. Everything was too hot and too claustrophobic. She raised herself with the intention of going to the window, but her ankle was worse than she thought and there was no way she would make it across the room.

So she lay on her covers instead. But the thought of Mr Hartley put an end to any plans she had of sleeping. That became one of the most uncomfortable nights Annabelle had ever experienced.

Chapter Twelve

"Does anyone fancy a trip to town?" Charles asked the breakfasters. A week had passed since the party, and the final guests had left Godshollow.

"Today?" Beatrice cast a quick look outside. "If I were a gambler, I would put money on it raining." Mr Daniels nodded in agreement.

"I think an outing would be lovely," Miss Knight spoke up. "There's no need to be scared of a little rain."

Charles' heart beat furiously against his chest when he realised he and Miss Knight might be going alone. He watched as Annabelle's uncle and chaperone came to the same conclusion.

"Hmm . . ." The older man narrowed his eyes. "Well, it will be your own faults if you get soaked through and catch a cold." He looked to the other members of the breakfast table.

"It won't rain," Charles answered confidently.

"Do you need me to accompany you?" Jasper asked, finally looking up from his paper.

He can't come with us! I'd rather ride through a storm!

"I'm sure your time would be better spent here. I'm sure Mr Daniels values your help." Once again, Beatrice's quick thinking had saved Charles.

Jasper hummed his approval. "Then you'd best take the curricle. It has the top, if it should rain. There's no need to take the carriage for just two people."

This plan is coming together quite nicely, Charles thought to himself. When he'd first mentioned the idea, he'd expected a group outing. Now, though, he was getting the chance to be alone with Miss Knight for as long as they wanted.

"Are you sure this is a good idea?" Beatrice had cornered Charles whilst he prepared the curricle.

"What do you mean?" Charles asked as he fastened the strap of the horse's harness.

"Stop being coy. You know exactly what I mean," his sister replied, her lips pursed. "Charles, you can't keep doing this without making a decision. It's not fair to Annabelle."

"It's not fair to me either." Charles moaned. "This is the happiest I've ever been. Jasper won't—"

"Oh, so what? Are you going to put her into a compromising position so that Jasper *has* to let you marry her?"

Charles' eyes lit up briefly at the idea

"*No*, Charles," Beatrice said firmly. "That would break her heart, and you know it!"

Charles guiltily dropped his gaze down to his feet. "What can I do?" he asked in anguish.

"Be a man and speak to Jasper. *Soon.*"

"That will end in disaster!"

"What will be a disaster? The trip? I don't think it will rain very much, if at all."

Miss Knight had chosen this moment to round the corner of the stables. She'd gone to her room for a coat and a bonnet, and her beautiful face was lit with excitement.

Charles' entire body tensed. *How much did she hear?* "N-nothing," he stuttered. "I'm ready to go if you are."

"More than ready."

The young woman beamed at him as he helped her onto the curricle. Charles didn't need to look behind him to know that Beatrice was watching him with her *motherly* gaze of warning.

"We'll see you later," he told her before she had a chance

to offer any more advice. He pulled on the reins, and the horses began to trot out of the courtyard.

The start of the journey began in silence. Charles was intensely aware of his heartbeat. He'd been so excited at the chance for a moment alone with Miss Knight, and now the moment was here, he was tongue-tied with nerves.

Damn Beatrice and her interfering.

He was sure he would've been fine if his sister hadn't tried to be logical and practical.

Charles watched Miss Knight from the corner of his eye. She seemed to be quite unable to find anything to say as well. He watched her delicate hands smooth the ribbon of her bonnet.

"I think—"

"Thank you—"

Both of them spoke at once.

"You first," Charles insisted. He heard Miss Knight take a deep breath and place her hands in her lap.

"Thank you for suggesting an outing," she said at length. "My ankle feels much better, and I think I might have gone mad if I'd stayed inside any longer."

Charles was shocked. "I'm glad you're feeling better, but I thought you loved Godshollow!"

"I do," Miss Knight assured him. "I just don't like having nothing to do." She sighed wistfully. "This has been the best time of my life, I've enjoyed it so much. I can't believe this all belongs to my uncle. If he stays, I'll be visiting whenever I can."

"You do seem much happier here than you were in Bath." He groaned softly. *Why had he said that!* "I'm sorry," he blurted out. "I didn't mean to—"

"No," Miss Knight said gently. "*I* should be sorry. I was so excited about Bath, but I ruined it."

"Ridiculous," Charles bit out harshly.

Miss Knight jumped in her seat next to him.

He put his hand on hers comfortingly. "*You* didn't do anything," he assured her with as much care as he could.

"To think this was all caused by my rejecting Mr Evans." She sighed bitterly. "I don't think he even liked me all that much. I'm certainly not worth all the effort he expended to spite me. He was just being childish."

"He was," Charles replied sincerely. "Though we will have to agree to disagree about what you're worth. I'm sorry you ever had to go through that."

"I'm still glad I refused him," she replied strongly.

"I am too." Charles had said it before he even realised. *Oh, Lord!*

"You—you are?" Her voice was so hopeful, it just about broke Charles' heart. He *had* to tell her how he felt. After saying that, how could he not?

He drew the curricle to a slow stop and swallowed hard. He turned towards his passenger, his heart racing. "Miss Knight." His voice sounded hoarse and broken even to his own ears. He picked up the lady's gloved hands and held them in his own.

Deep breath, Charles. Just tell her she is the most wonderful person you've ever met. It's not that hard.

He breathed in through his nose. His stomach was threatening a revolt. As he looked down at their joined hands, he couldn't tell which of them was causing the shaking.

"Miss Knight," he repeated again. He licked his lips, which were suddenly dryer than a desert.

The beautiful creature next to him watched him with eyes as big as saucers. Charles heard her breaths come out in fast gasps.

Then she squealed. A fat raindrop had fallen onto the bridge of her nose. No sooner had it landed then it was joined by thousands of its kin. The heavens opened and a large crack of thunder pealed across the sky. They were soaked before they had the chance to even *think* about pulling the top over them.

"We'll have to turn back," Charles shouted over the horrendous din of the raindrops. "The town is too far away. God, I hate it when Beatrice is right!"

Beside him, instead of screaming like any other woman in her position would do, Miss Knight was laughing hysterically.

"You're mad!" Charles cried to her as he turned the curricle around. They were jolted forward as one of the wheels slipped on the wet road.

"You have to admit, it's a little funny." The young woman laughed as she tipped her head up, directly into the heavy shower of water.

Charles couldn't help but chuckle at her outlandish enthusiasm. This woman was incredible. *Who else would be happy to be caught in a rainstorm?*

He drove the horses as fast as they could go. The rain continued to beat steadily down on them, and mud splashed up the sides of the carriage. They were a mess by the time Godshollow appeared in sight.

"Thank goodness!" Miss Knight cried.

They were both becoming cold and uncomfortable. The initial humour over the situation had waned, and they both whooped with relief as they gained the cover of the courtyard.

Charles helped Miss Knight from the curricle and guided them into a small shelter while the groom took the horses back to the stable. Both of them were wet through. Charles found himself gazing at Annabelle, at the patches of her dress where the fabric had become translucent due to the rainwater. The dress clung to her curves, and the image caused a stirring within him, stronger than he'd experienced before. He looked up and noticed a smudge of dirt on her face and saw an opportunity.

The courtyard was deserted. It seemed that the household

was smart enough not to attempt to go outside. Beatrice had been right when she said that compromising Miss Knight would break her heart. But, if he didn't do something now, he was sure he would perish.

He stepped forward so that he was mere inches from her, and she was pressed gently against the wall. "Hold still," he whispered quietly. He raised his hand to her eye level and slowly took off his glove, teasing her with it. He watched as her eyes were transfixed to his fingers and followed them as they drew closer to her face.

As his thumb reached across her cheek to rub the dirt away, she tore her gaze from his hand and into his eyes. Seeing the look therein, Charles felt faint. Her eyes held a hunger and passion that was overwhelming and tempting, and there was nothing else Charles could do.

He leaned in, pressing her against the wall, their bodies now flush. Charles shivered when her dainty hands came to rest on his biceps. Her sweet pink tongue darted out to lick at her lips and Charles lost all composure.

"Annabelle," he murmured, his voice low and full of desire. With that one word he was letting her know his deepest wants, asking for permission to act on his dreams. He *had* to use her first name. He cupped her face and searched her eyes for permission to end his torment.

After what seemed like an eternity, she answered him. The word yes fell with a sigh from her lips, acquiescing to everything he was asking for.

His heart soared and he wasted no time in closing the small distance between them, pressing his lips to hers. Not a hard, demanding kiss, but not soft either. The kiss was full of need and desire—two people giving in to what they'd been denying themselves.

He felt Annabelle kiss him back, and that spurred him on. His hand on her face moved around to cradle the back of her neck, while he curled the other about her, stopping where the ribbon of her dress lightly brushed against his skin, the delicate sensation setting his nerves alight. He pressed her even closer against him, letting her feel not just the desire in his kiss, but in his body as well.

His skin tingled, and he'd never felt so alive. Her small frame was crushed between the wall and himself, and she fit against him as though she was made for him. His hands roamed over her body, the flimsy, wet cotton of her dress providing little barrier between them.

His lips travelled from hers, up her neck and to her ear.

"Tell me to stop," he whispered, struggling to breathe. Her soft curls enveloped him, threatening to drown him.

He felt Annabelle shake her head. Charles growled hungrily and attacked her lips with renewed fervour. She moaned into his mouth and held herself against him, driving him mad.

"Mr Hartley." Her voice was hoarse and needy. Her fingers dug into his shoulders as she clung to him.

"Call me Charles," he demanded against her skin. She gasped as he dipped his head lower to kiss the top of her décolletage.

"Charles!"

Wait. That wasn't Annabelle's voice.

"Annabelle?"

Definitely not.

"Are you out here? You'll catch your death of cold."

Beatrice.

Charles jolted. Annabelle was frozen against him. Beatrice's footstep drew ever closer.

Charles pressed one last kiss against Annabelle's lips then stepped backwards. He took deep gulps of air, trying to calm himself.

Annabelle was smoothing the front of her dress. They both stared at each other in silence.

Charles couldn't discern the look on Annabelle's face. Her

eyes were wide, and her chest was heaving. Her mouth hung open slightly. He stepped forward with an arm out towards her.

"Annabelle —"

"There you are." Beatrice came barrelling around the corner. "What are you doing out here? I told you it was going to rain." As Charles' sister came upon them, she stopped. Charles panicked as her focus passed from one of them to the other. He could hear her brain trying to put the pieces together.

Her eyes narrowed and her lips formed a thin line.

Charles gulped.

"Annabelle, dear, you're shaking."

Charles felt like an absolute cad as he realised the truth of his sister's words. Poor Annabelle had been soaked to the bone, and while she might have warmed up as they kissed, she was now cold and shivering. Charles reached for her, but Beatrice got there first. He could only watch as Annabelle was led inside.

Charles ran a hand through his hair and blew a hard breath into the air. His body still tingled. He could still feel her against him. That kiss had been unlike anything he'd ever encountered before. There was no way he could let her go.

He had to speak to Jasper. *Now.*

Charles had marched into the house, not even bothering to change out of his sodden clothes. But now he was stood in front of his brother's door, fist poised ready to knock on the wood, and he couldn't bring himself to complete the action.

His stomach twisted horribly.

You shouldn't be this scared of your own brother, his mind chastised. *It's very simple. You love her. You want to marry her. Don't ask Jasper, tell him.*

"That's easy for you to say," he mumbled under his breath.

He steeled himself and made ready to knock on the door, but it was pulled open before he could do anything.

"Just come in, will you. Stop standing around like a fool."

Jasper ushered Charles into the room and pointed to a chair in the corner.

"What do you want?" his brother asked with a bored tone.

Charles sat in the seat, twisting his wet coat in his hands. Then he stood abruptly. Then he sat back down. When he stood again and began to pace, Jasper huffed.

"I *am* busy, you know," he snipped. "What's wrong with you?"

Charles took a deep breath. He felt like a naughty child.

"IwanttomarryMissKnight." His statement came out in a rushed jumble of words. Charles looked at his brother warily.

Jasper sighed, clearly annoyed. Charles braced himself for the argument.

"For goodness sake," the elder brother huffed. "I thought this would be about something important."

Charles blanched. "W–What?" he stammered.

"Look," Jasper snapped. "I have more serious matters to deal with. Try not to be a complete imbecile."

Charles felt as though he'd been thrown against a tree. "You — you're fine with it?"

Why are you arguing? His mind screamed. *Take it and run.*

Jasper sighed once again and gestured towards the chair. He waited in silence for Charles to sit down.

"It has been quite clear to me you have feelings for Miss Knight. I'd hoped you'd get over it, but I see you haven't."

Charles nodded dumbly.

"If I'd been in any doubt, your little performance in the stables — which I can see from my room by the way — certainly set me straight."

Charles groaned and embarrassment curled tight in his chest. "You consent?" he murmured, still not quite sure what was happening.

"Yes, you dolt," Jasper replied. "I'd been holding out for a more financially prudent marriage for you. But there's little that can be done now. I shall have to focus my efforts on Beatrice."

Poor girl was Charles' first thought. Quickly, his mind returned to the present. "You're saying I *can marry Annabelle?*" he uttered in amazement.

"Yes," Jasper answered as though he was speaking to a child. "Has being in love made you slow? Well, go on then."

"I can't marry her right now!"

Jasper pressed a hand to his forehead and gave Charles a small shove with the other.

"No, you can't," the man said slowly. "But you can ask her uncle for her hand."

With that, Jasper pushed Charles through the door and slammed it behind him.

Mr Daniels met Charles' request with yet more surprising behaviour.

"Well, it's about time! I was starting to worry it would never happen." The old man chuckled. "Give me a few days to write to her parents."

As Charles left the study, he heard Mr Daniels laugh to himself. "I owe Miss Hartley ten shillings."

CHAPTER THIRTEEN

Annabelle sank into the warm water of the bath in the privacy of her room. She could still feel the pressure of Charles' lips against hers, the urgency with which his hands had touched her. Her head was swimming.

The way he'd held her had made her body tingle. It had awakened her in a way she'd never experienced before. She was sure, in that instant, she could feel every nerve in her body. His strong arms had encased her and pulled her closer to him. She'd been so close she could have counted the individual lashes that framed the intensely deep blue eyes she so often found herself gazing at.

She had loved it. That was easily the most passionate moment of her life.

She knew, deep down, she shouldn't be rejoicing in such inappropriate behaviour, but how could she not? That had been just so perfect. All her life she'd read about romantic trysts like this, and now she was living one.

Charles Hartley is not a tryst!

Of course he wasn't. What she felt for him wasn't pure passion alone. She wasn't like the young Penelope, lusting after Peter in *Fantasising about the Farm Boy*.

She loved the way he made her laugh, the way he teased her when she was being silly, and the other times when he spoke so gently to her. Everything he did made her feel she wanted to spend the rest of her life making him happy.

She couldn't deny it to herself any longer — she loved him. She was sure of it.

And now, she was pretty sure he cared for her too.

She giggled girlishly as she sank deeper into the water.

You kissed him. He kissed you! And what a kiss it had been.

Her heart was doing somersaults. She giggled again, which turned into a full-body laugh. She sent splashes of water over the edges of the bathtub.

A knock at the door reminded her where she was. For a second, she thought it might be Mr Hartley coming to kiss her again. But a different Hartley voice came from the other side of the door.

"Annabelle?" — it was Beatrice — "I'm having tea in the third drawing room. You know, the one with the blue paper. Join me when you're finished."

"I will."

Annabelle began to rub her arms and legs, helping the water to warm her. When she was finished, she dried herself quickly and dressed with the help of the maid Beatrice had found for her.

Her friend was curled in an armchair, reading a Fanny Sparrow novel, when Annabelle entered. Her green eyes twinkled happily as they settled on Annabelle.

"Feeling warmer?" Beatrice asked convivially.

"Definitely," Annabelle replied as she took her own seat. "You were right about the rain." Annabelle was trying to make conversation, but she was still too preoccupied with thoughts of the kiss.

Beatrice hummed lightly. "I'm never wrong." She laughed, but Annabelle remained silent.

"Did anything interesting happen on your trip?" Beatrice asked, letting Annabelle know she hadn't spoken for a while.

Annabelle felt the flush rise on her cheeks, and she tried to keep her voice level. "Not particularly." She hoped she sounded convincing to Beatrice — in her own head, she certainly didn't.

"Ah."

Annabelle looked up when the other girl grew quiet. Beatrice was pretending to read her book, her eyes fixed on the same place, her fingers turning the pages far too quickly. Eventually, she sighed and put the book down on the table.

"You would tell me, if anything *did* happen?" Beatrice asked.

Guilt twisted in Annabelle's stomach. She wanted nothing more than to tell her about the kiss, but she wanted to speak to Charles first.

"Of course," she answered, hoping her voice didn't give her away.

Beatrice nodded and lifted her teacup to her lips. "Oh!" she announced suddenly, sending ripples across the surface of the hot liquid. "A letter came for you while you were out." Beatrice pulled a small envelope out of her pocket and handed it to Annabelle.

Any happy emotion Annabelle had been feeling vanished as she read the neat cursive that covered the paper.

Annabelle,

Significant time has passed since your leaving Bath. And in that time, I have been able to reflect on what passed between us.

I have decided that I can forgive you.

I know that you never meant to cause us any harm. I realise now that Gregory's proposal could have been a shock to you. It did not escape my notice how young and naïve you are. It may be that you weren't aware of your inappropriate actions.

I suspect that Gregory will recover from the insult, given time.

Carys.

Gwen had scribbled a note underneath.

Please don't blame Gregory for his actions. He just loved you so much. He never meant to drive you away. I know you are a good, Christian girl and I know that what was done was done for love. With friendship, Gwen.

"Annabelle?" Beatrice was at her side—she must have

moved whilst Annabelle was reading the letter.

"Carys says she has forgiven me," Annabelle cried incredulously. She threw the paper down furiously and let out a spiteful laugh. "After everything they've done, she believes that *she* is the one in the position to be forgiving." She scoffed again. "I'm sorry, but that's unbelievable! She says I'm young and naïve so she can forgive me for being so foolish because I knew no better." She put her head in her hands and sighed angrily. She was unable to stop the tears.

Beatrice put her arm around Annabelle. "I'm sorry," she said sincerely. "This is a truly horrible situation, and you have a right to be upset. *They're* the ones who have abused *your* kindness and *your* friendship. They've treated you very poorly, and they have no right to ask you for forgiveness or to say you are forgiven." She patted her friend's hand. "You are not naïve either, of that I'm certain. You're young, yes. And perhaps idealistic. But there's nothing wrong with that. I think what you did was brave, not foolish. You're young, you don't have to settle for the first man who asks for you.

"Maybe when you get to be my age, it might be different," she joked. "But for now, you're at a time in your life where you can chase love if you want to. Don't let anyone tell you otherwise, or make you feel differently."

Annabelle lifted her head and sniffled. "My uncle says I made the right decision," she mumbled quietly. "But everyone else says I've been unforgivably stupid."

Beatrice huffed angrily beside her. "Right. Come with me." She grabbed hold of Annabelle's hand and pulled her out of her seat. The young girl had no choice but to follow as her friend determinedly led her down a hallway.

As the girls marched through Godshollow, they happened upon Charles as he was leaving Mr Daniels' room. He smiled as he saw Annabelle, making her heart flutter. But she knew the instant he noticed her sad demeanour — the smile dropped into a frown.

"What's the matter?" he asked as Beatrice barrelled past him with Annabelle.

"Is Mr Daniels in there?" Beatrice asked, not waiting for the answer before pushing the door open.

"Yes," Charles replied, confused. "But what—"

The three young people crowded into Mr Daniels' room. The old man's face lit up when he saw his niece.

"Annabelle, my dear," he exclaimed happily with a peculiar grin. As he took in her face, he became more serious. "Whatever's the matter, my love?" he asked concerned.

Whilst her temperament was now a lot calmer, Annabelle's face was still red and blotchy, clearly indicating she'd been crying, and betrayed her considerable distress. She still had the letters clutched in her grip and passed them over to Mr Daniels.

Beatrice spoke up. "I need your help to convince Annabelle that she hasn't done anything wrong."

Mr Daniels read the letter in silence. His face was grave when he looked up at Annabelle. "This is outrageous." His voice was calm and measured, but his face was set in a grimace and Annabelle knew the anger that was within him. "I will definitely be having a word with my wife about this. This has gone too far."

"No!" Annabelle cried, panicked. "If you send her a letter, they will probably see it too. Who knows what will happen if they think we're scolding them?"

Annabelle felt Beatrice grip her hand tighter in comfort.

"That won't be necessary," Mr Daniels said with a weary sigh. "A letter arrived for me today. Moira will be joining us tomorrow."

Annabelle couldn't stop the gasp that fell from her lips.

Mr Daniels moved around the room and swept his niece into his arms.

"She will be under strict instructions not to talk about Mr Evans," he told the top of her head. "I promise."

"Is she still mad at me?" Annabelle sniffled against his shoulder.

"If she is, she has no right to be so," Mr Daniels uttered. "And I will let her know that." He sighed sadly and released Annabelle from the hug so he could look straight in her face. "We've heard the last from the Evanses. He was rude and obnoxious, and I pity any girl he may marry." He gave Annabelle a pat on the cheek. "Now, off you go. Go and find out what extraordinary delights Miss Sparrow has concocted this week. I need to write to your parents."

Annabelle had no time to question why her parents needed to be written to as she was bundled out the door with the Hartleys.

"You see?" Beatrice cajoled her as they stood in the hallway. "Rude and obnoxious. Definitely not the man for you."

Annabelle sniffled and rubbed her eyes. "He doesn't even read novels," she said with a tired laugh.

"There we go, then," Beatrice replied firmly. "Any man who doesn't read novels is not worth your time. Now, let's see if we can convince Charles to read us the new instalment of Arturo Avalon."

The girls propositioned the gentleman, who agreed readily. He took Annabelle's arm as Beatrice marched off towards the drawing room.

"Are you all right?" His voice was low and concerned.

Annabelle was reminded that not even an hour earlier, he'd been pressed up against her in the courtyard.

"Yes," she answered softly. Her body felt as though it was on fire. She struggled hard to maintain her composure.

"Good." He paused for a moment, staring straight in front of him. Then he chuckled nervously. "When I saw you with Beatrice, and I saw you'd been crying . . ." Annabelle saw a blush creep up his face. "I thought you were crying about our kiss."

Now it was Annabelle's turn to be embarrassed. She stammered uncontrollably. "No! Not–Never–I–It–"

Charles breathed a sigh of relief, and a goofy smile curled his lips. That smile sent hundreds of flutters into Annabelle's stomach. "Thank goodness," he breathed. "I'd hate to think I was such a bad kisser that I made you cry."

Annabelle laughed and swatted Charles on the forearm.

Charles chuckled too, and then he became serious. He stopped in the hallway and faced Annabelle. "I have to speak with you alone," he told her, his deep voice full of emotion.

Annabelle's head began to swim. "We–we're alone now," she whispered, her hands shaking.

"So we are." Charles took a step towards her. His eyes held the same gaze they had when he'd kissed her in the courtyard. Her mouth went dry and her lips tingled.

"Are you two coming?" Beatrice called from the drawing room. "We have a visitor!"

Annabelle sighed, then laughed.

"I'll wait until we can't be interrupted," Charles told her.

"But that is a talent of hers," Annabelle joked. Though, at that moment, she felt like strangling her best friend.

"I will see you later," Charles promised. Then he placed a gentle kiss on her cheek and walked away.

Annabelle was exhausted. This day had been a see-saw of intense emotion, and she'd been drained of the majority of her energy. But she was intrigued to see who their visitor was.

"Mrs Lutton!" she cried happily when she found the older woman in the drawing room.

"Hello, my dear. I hope you don't mind me paying a visit. I did send a note, though your surprise would suggest that you never got it."

Annabelle hugged the general's wife. "Of course not," she

assured her. "It's lovely to see you."

"A surprise is always welcome," Beatrice added with a smile. "Though I fear we are wholly unprepared. I'll fetch us some tea."

When Beatrice had left the room, Mrs Lutton turned her sharp eyes to Anabelle.

"So tell me," the old woman said with a devious smile. "How goes your pursuit of the younger Hartley gentleman?"

Annabelle froze. Her amused laughter was replaced with silence and a deep surprise she could feel down to her toes. She gaped at her companion.

"Come now, dear," Mrs Lutton said. "Don't be embarrassed. The two of you would be a very good match. It's perfectly reasonable that your head would be turned by such a man. Besides, it's obvious you both think very highly of each other, and he clearly cares for you."

"But you've only seen us together once." Annabelle's heart beat frantically against her chest.

"Well . . ." Mrs Lutton shrugged nonchalantly. "Even a blind person could see the connection between you."

"I quite agree," Beatrice announced as she returned to the drawing room. She put a tray down on the table and began to pour tea. "However, I fear we're embarrassing Annabelle. Mrs Lutton, tell us about your romance with the general."

The old woman tipped her head back and laughed. "Now *that* is a tale."

The younger girls listened expectantly.

"Some time after the death of my first husband, my daughter fell in with a young man by the name of Frederick Lutton. She admits that it was an awful match. They had nothing in common, and he was most certainly in it for the money. My late husband, though he gave me neither love nor kindness, did, on his death, leave me with a sizable fortune.

"Needless to say, their courtship didn't last. He found a

substantially wealthier lady to woo, but during their two-year flirtation, I developed a very close and eventually intimate relationship with the young man's father, who is now my current husband."

Annabelle gasped in delight upon the story's conclusion. "How wonderful," she exclaimed. "How romantic!"

Mrs Lutton laughed. "My daughter certainly didn't think it so. She felt humiliated and condemned our relationship, even going so far as to say I'd betrayed her. She refused to attend the wedding, and, despite my numerous letters of entreaty, she has declined to acknowledge me since, even though she's now happily married and has a daughter of her own." The older lady shook her head. "She's a stubborn girl, but I can't be angry, as I know she's inherited that particular trait from me."

The ladies continued to talk well into the evening. But Annabelle grew more anxious the longer they conversed.

She could only think of Charles' promise that he would talk to her. Alone. The thought made her shiver excitedly. But as the night wore on, Annabelle was concerned she would have to wait until the morning.

This seemed a more and more likely scenario. When Annabelle went to bed, still not having talked to Charles, she was beside herself with nerves.

She tried to read her book to relax but not even *The Magical Miss Maris* and her supernatural adventures could distract her. She was so restless she had to get up. She paced around her room before she decided she needed a more substantial walk.

She headed for the tower they'd found on their first proper day. She hoped the gothic wonder of the room might distract her. Decided, she wrapped herself in a housecoat, picked up her candle and her book—in case she really couldn't sleep anywhere—and set off.

CHAPTER FOURTEEN

Annabelle tiptoed carefully through the house so as not to wake anyone. Heavy velvet curtains covered the large windows, creating a thick darkness in the hallways. She hoped she knew the route well enough by now not to get lost.

She crept through the halls and up the antique staircase, finally finding the right door. She pushed it open and entered the tiny attic tower. She held her candle aloft, and it cast long shadows around the room. Annabelle loved this room in the daytime, but seeing it in the dark, by candlelight, she fell in love with it even more. The gothic feel of the place wrapped around her, exciting every nerve.

There was also a tension in the air, and for a while, Annabelle jumped at every little noise and gust of wind as she walked about the room. Eventually she calmed, convincing herself it was just the old building, moving and settling. She'd convinced herself of this so fully she didn't notice approaching footsteps until their owner announced himself with a cough.

She whirled around to face him, his name escaping her lips in a gasp. The shock caused her to drop her candle. It fell to the floor and plunged the room into darkness. She stood stock still for a moment, trying to take in her surroundings and adjust to the low light. Then she gently called out. "Ch–Charles?" A small silence followed, and she felt him move behind her.

"Annabelle."

The word was a low murmur, tantalisingly close to her ear.

160

Heat rose to her face at his proximity. If she took a step back, she'd probably find herself flush against his chest. The thought was very tempting. She felt the light press of his fingers creep daringly up the top of her arm and over her shoulder, tucking her hair behind it.

"I'm sorry I didn't find you earlier," he said gently. "By the time Mrs Lutton finally left, I was told you'd gone to bed. Please don't think I was reneging on my promise."

"I didn't," she replied softly.

"But now," he continued, so close to her he was driving Annabelle crazy. "Now I find you in the tower. What are you doing in here, Annabelle? What has you up at such a late hour? This is surely too late for young ladies to be roaming the halls."

She turned to face him. He plucked the book from her grip.

"I see," he chuckled quietly. "This is one of your beloved Fanny Sparrow novels, am I right? Were you looking for some gothic horrors?" His voice was teasing, though not in the usual way — this was a sultry and seductive teasing. "Are you looking for ghosts? Monsters, perhaps?"

He paused dramatically, took a step closer to her. "Some dreadful midnight secret?" He whispered low and close to her ear, pressing the book back into her hands.

"Oh Charles, you must stop teasing me," Annabelle cried. Her voice came out less confident than she'd hoped. She heard it reverberate around the small room. In truth, being this close to Charles was having such an effect on her she could barely control her heartbeat let alone her voice. A thrill ran through her entire body.

Charles gave a small laugh and raised her hand to his lips. He pressed a gentle kiss against her knuckles. "Please accept my sincerest apologies," he whispered.

He placed another kiss at the tips of her fingers. "It's just so tempting," he added.

Annabelle sighed gently. His closeness was sending wonderful tingles through her body and she found she couldn't open her mouth to say anything.

Charles released her hand to fall softly back to her side. "Now," he said, suddenly breaking the heavy silence as he starting to move about the room. "Why are you in here? Why are you creeping around the house alone?" His warm breath blew against her ear and cheek. A shiver ran the length of her body. "Were you hoping to get caught?"

She turned to face him, her eyes searching his in an attempt to find a reasonable excuse. In the end she gave up. "Perhaps," she conceded, her voice quiet and embarrassed. "I just . . . I couldn't sleep. I thought it might help . . . Wanted to calm my mind . . . I thought you'd all be asleep."

"Calm your mind?" he enquired in an intrigued tone. "What have you been thinking about that's stopped you from sleeping? I don't wish to seem arrogant or presumptuous, but would I be right in hoping some of those thoughts are about me?"

Without looking up, Annabelle nodded gently. "You know very well they are."

Even in the darkness, Annabelle could see his bright eyes light up. He moved a hand to gently rest against her face, pulling her gaze up to his.

"Then," he began slowly, tracing the line of her cheek with his finger. "I'll forgive you your midnight wonderings, my dear Annabelle, if . . . ." He paused. Annabelle looked at him expectantly. "If you grant me another kiss."

Annabelle gasped, the tiny sound echoing around the room. She clutched the front of his nightshirt.

He spoke again, his voice low and quiet and urgent. "Please, Annabelle" — his tone bordered on pleading — "that kiss we shared is all I can think of. It haunts my every thought. Dear, sweet Annabelle, I am consumed."

How should she respond to such a plea?

The hunger with which he spoke to her left her weak. That she, plain she, occupied his thoughts set her soul ablaze with joy. How could she refuse him?

But you must!

But I can't!

But it is improper!

To hell with propriety!

She gazed into his intense eyes and knew. She leaned up, balancing on her tiptoes and drew her face closer to him.

She closed the gap between them and pressed herself to him, her lips meeting his in a joyous union.

His joy was evident. He threw his arms around her and practically lifted her off the floor. His lips left a trail of elated kisses from her mouth, down her neck and back up to claim her lips once again in a scorching kiss. He was hungry and needing, but not demanding or harsh. Annabelle answered with as much force as she could, pouring all her love and desire into him. She felt safe in his arms.

The kiss came to its natural conclusion, both of them left breathless. Charles pulled back slightly to rest his forehead against Annabelle's. He whispered her name. It fell from his lips like one of his prayers. His fingertips played with the neckline on her shoulder, tracing the line of the strap. Annabelle could feel his breath coming fast against her face, almost matching the speed of her own. She heard him take a deep breath and swallow audibly. After what seemed like an eternity in the dark, he spoke.

"This isn't how I intended this to go," he spoke gently and quietly, his voice full of apology. "I'd planned it so many ways . . . you deserve better than this. But I can't go another moment, Annabelle, without knowing." He took her hand and led her to the window that they might be able to see more clearly. He raised his hand to touch her face but clearly became nervous and thought better of the idea, returning his hand to his lap.

"Annabelle," he began. "From the moment you ran into me at that ball in Bath, you're the one who has occupied my thoughts." He took her hands in his and gazed deep into her eyes, as though he was trying to convey everything he was unable to say through them.

He took another deep breath and continued. "Annabelle, I hope this doesn't seem too forward or too surprising. I hope I can't be mistaken that you return my feelings at least in part, or this is going to be incredibly awkward.

"But please know I love you. I feel as if I'm bound to you, in ways I scarcely thought possible. I've known all my life there were plans for me with regards to my marriage. I was *destined* for an heiress or duchess." He shook his head, grasping her hands tighter. "But until I met you, I didn't realise exactly what a marriage of convenience meant I was giving up. I thought that was how marriages were, that only fictional characters get to marry for love. But you've given me hope, and I don't know if I have the strength to relinquish it."

He stopped, once again searching her eyes.

"What are you saying Charles?" Annabelle asked, overcome with the emotion of his declaration. Her heart was pounding wildly, but she was terrified she misunderstood him.

He moved his hand, this time resting it against the curve of her cheek, each fingertip like a blazing fire against Annabelle's skin.

"What I'm saying, Annabelle. Dearest Annabelle. Pure, wonderful, beautiful Annabelle. Is that I want to marry you. I've spoken to my brother, and though he'd rather a marriage of connections, I've told him I can do nothing else."

Annabelle could feel Charles' hands shaking as he continued. "I'll do anything and everything to make you happy and to be the man you deserve. I know I can't rival the men in your novels, but I also know it's not possible for me to love you with any more of my heart. It's all yours." He pressed her hand against his chest and waited for her to respond. "Marry me, Annabelle," he half-whispered, his voice almost desperate.

Annabelle was overwhelmed. This was the second proposal she'd received in as many months, though the two didn't compare at all. The words each man had used, the way in which they were delivered, definitely set this one above the other, but this was one she had only dreamt of until this moment. She was speechless, her mind swimming. She tried to gather her thoughts, aware that the longer she remained silent, the more suspense and pain she was causing to Charles.

"I know you're not the hero from one of my novels," she began slowly, reaching up to touch the lips she'd kissed mere moments before. "That's *not* what I want. Men like that don't exist, and I don't expect you to be such. I don't *want* you to be. But I don't think they're the only ones who can marry for love." She clutched his hands tight and brought them to her lips to bestow a kiss upon them.

"I know you'll make me happy, Charles. I don't know if you realise just how happy you've made me already. The way you treat me, it's more than I deserve. I know that by the nature of my position in society, I deserve nothing from you. And while you've occupied my every waking thought as well, the idea that you returned my affections was something I'd only entertained in my deepest dreams. That kiss we shared today was one of the best moments of my life, but I feared nothing more should come of it. I'm aware of my low birth, but if you're willing to look past that, I'll give whatever is in my power to make you happy. I love you. Of *course,* I will marry you."

She was so overjoyed to be uttering these words she was near laughing.

A wide smile broke across Charles' face as well as he let out a pent-up breath. He leaned forward and kissed her passionately. With unprecedented foresight, given his state of euphoria, he'd cradled the back of her head with his hand to stop the force of the kiss from banging her head into the window frame.

He showered her with kisses, covering her lips, her face, and her neck. "Oh Annabelle," he sighed, almost a moan. "My darling, how I've longed to hear those words, you can't know."

He pulled back slightly to look into her face. "I spoke with your uncle, and he was sure of your parents' approval. He's already written them on the matter." He beamed at her in the darkness.

So that's what he meant earlier. The thought only had the merest of seconds to enter her mind before Charles ensured that she couldn't think at all.

He kissed her again, deeper this time, and he took her by the arms. She looked into his eyes and saw burning desire, something she knew was reflected in her own.

"How long?" she asked, hoping her voice came out strong and seductive, though in actuality, it was more breathless and shaky.

He kissed her neck, up along her jaw, and to her ear. "Since Bath," he admitted passionately. "That party. When everyone was gossiping. The thought of you with anyone else made me sick. I'm so glad you refused that damned Welshman."

"Me too," Annabelle whispered huskily. He wrapped his arms tighter around her.

"Annabelle," he moaned. His voice sent shivers through her.

He kissed the hollow of her neck, leaving a scorching trail along her skin. One arm strongly wrapped around her waist, he began to push the shoulder of her nightgown away, exposing more of her skin for his hungry lips. His hand trailed down.

Annabelle cried his name, her voice taking on a tone she'd never heard before, full of need and lust. She might have said more, but her voice was lost as Charles' lips followed the path of his hand, worshipping her soft, pale skin. She leaned into his touch, arching her back, keeping a tight grip on his shoulders. He released her and lavished her with kisses. Annabelle groaned softly at the loss but was again struck dumb as he declared his thoughts against her skin.

"You are divine."

In that moment, she'd never felt more beautiful. Annabelle lifted Charles' chin to claim his mouth in a hungry kiss, pouring her heart out through her lips. He moaned into her mouth as her hands began to roam his chest, his night shirt providing only the flimsiest of barriers. He shifted a little and groaned again. The movement sent sparks through Annabelle's body.

"Annabelle," he whispered once more, her name a declaration of love. Charles seemed taken over by his lust and was trying to get her as close to him as possible. This completely threw Annabelle's balance, sending them both to the floor, tangled together.

Once over the initial shock, they both laughed.

"Are you all right?" Charles asked, flustered.

Annabelle nodded, too winded and laughing too much to give a verbal response. She found she was quite enjoying their current position. It was like her dream of the waterfall. His arms were either side of her head, holding his weight from her. But he *was* touching her. The length of his body was pressed deliciously against hers.

Eventually, after a few more slow kisses, he stood and helped her to her feet. He gazed at her for a few moments.

"Perhaps we should go to bed," he suggested.

Annabelle couldn't prevent her expression of pure shock.

"Not together, I mean," he added hastily. "Separately. I'm not that dishonourable." He smiled sheepishly, as though he was embarrassed for getting carried away. He replaced the shoulder of her dress where it was still out of place, then wrapped his arm around her, pulling her close.

"Good night, Annabelle." He gave her another kiss, leaving her tingling and ablaze with feeling.

Charles was in a daze.

An invisible force must have guided him to bed, because he was sure his feet weren't touching the floor.

I'm engaged! His mind shouted with joy. *To Annabelle*!

He felt like crying loud to the heavens of his bliss, but even in such ecstasy, he was mindful that most of the house was still asleep.

He lay on his bed, fully clothed, staring at the ceiling. His body throbbed.

What a day it had been.

"I'm engaged," he whispered disbelievingly into the night. "She said yes!" He laughed happily.

If only I had taken Beatrice's advice sooner. Had he known how Jasper was going to react, he would have gone to him much earlier.

Though, perhaps him seeing you kissing her senseless near the stables settled the matter for him.

He laughed again in disbelief. What a succession of events had occurred! Fanny Sparrow couldn't have come up with anything more outrageous.

But nobody else's opinions mattered. Because *she* had said yes. She was going to marry him. He was going to spend the rest of his life with her.

He felt stupefied.

As he drifted to sleep, images of Annabelle filled his head. She would kiss him and love him. Though his favourite dream by far was when she said *I do*.

Chapter Fifteen

Annabelle was as happy as it was possible for her to be. When she woke the next morning, her body and mind were still humming from the night before.

She wasn't sure what had happened wasn't all a dream. She could still feel his lips on her skin, but she'd had such wonderful dreams in the past. She finally accepted that everything was true when she realised she couldn't find her book. She must've left it in the tower room — which meant that everything last night *had* truly happened, and she was now engaged.

Her first job was to find her uncle. She raced happily through Godshollow and hammered on his door.

"Uncle! It's Annabelle. I must speak with you!"

"One moment." When he opened the door, he was bleary-eyed and had clearly just awakened, but he happily received Annabelle.

"This is an early hour for you," he commented cheerily.

"I know, I'm sorry." Annabelle rubbed her foot on the carpet guiltily. "I'm just so excited."

Mr Daniels laughed. "I can see that. Has Miss Sparrow announced a new series?" The question sounded sincere, but Annabelle could see her uncle was teasing her. He grinned widely. "Did he ask?"

Annabelle squealed with delight and threw herself into her uncle's arms.

"I'll take that as a yes, then," he chuckled as he hugged her. "I'm so happy for you, my dear. I couldn't approve more wholeheartedly. And I'm sure your parents will feel the same. I'm sure you're even gladder now that you turned down that Evans chap. I certainly am. Oh, I knew something would happen for the two of you, I'm so happy."

Mention of Mr Evans reminded Annabelle of her aunt's impending arrival. She bit her lip with agitation.

"Will Aunt Moira be angry with me?"

Her uncle put his hands on her shoulders. "As I said yesterday, she has no right to be." He gave her a playful tap under her chin. "She may be a little disappointed, but I shall let you in on a secret." He looked about him conspiratorially and Annabelle laughed. "I love my wife dearly, but she can—on occasion—be a bit silly."

Annabelle giggled and kissed her uncle on the cheek.

"Don't worry my dear," he told her. "I'm sure she just wants you to be happy, but if you want, I can tell her the news. She should be arriving soon. Now go and find Miss Hartley and tell her the good news."

As Annabelle raced off to find Beatrice, she ran into her new fiancé.

Fiancé! Ah!

He greeted her with a warm, jubilant smile.

"Good morning," he said giddily.

"Good morning," Annabelle replied, unable to stop the grin that spread across her face.

"I trust you had a pleasant night?"

Annabelle blushed to the roots of her hair. "It was most enjoyable," she answered coyly.

She squealed happily when Charles swept her into his arms and kissed her exuberantly.

"I was just going to inform my sister of some very happy news. Perhaps, you might be going the same way?"

"You read my mind." Annabelle slipped her arm into the crook of his elbow.

Beatrice's room wasn't far from Mr Daniels' in the grand

scheme of things. But the journey there took considerably longer than usual, as Charles seemed to grasp every opportunity he could find to kiss Annabelle. She definitely wasn't complaining.

They finally arrived at Beatrice's door and knocked for entry.

"Come in," Beatrice called brightly. Annabelle laughed when her friend cheerfully greeted Charles and then, bewildered, greeted her as well.

"Good morning, you two," she greeted suspiciously. "I trust you both had a good night?"

Annabelle squeaked with laughter and Beatrice seemed to quickly grasp the situation. She gazed between the two of them until Charles nodded.

"Finally!" Beatrice cried, hugging first Charles, then Annabelle. Then she swatted Charles on the shoulder. "You were certainly very slow," she teased. She turned to Annabelle. "And you said yes?"

"I did," Annabelle affirmed with a shy smile.

"Ah! This is wonderful!" Beatrice squealed happily. "I must inform Mrs Lutton at once."

"Mrs Lutton?" Charles asked. Annabelle giggled at his confused expression.

"Oh, yes," Beatrice replied happily. "The old dear was hoping there was something between you. She'll be so pleased. She'll take full credit and expect an invitation to the wedding, of course."

"*Of course.*" Charles wrapped his arms around Annabelle's shoulders. "As long as my fiancée agrees."

"Absolutely," Annabelle replied cheerfully. She twisted her neck and pressed a kiss to Charles' cheek.

Beatrice cleared her throat, reminding them she was there.

"You have *got* to stop doing that," he told his sister. Annabelle looked over her shoulder at her friend.

"Doing what?" Beatrice asked innocently.

"Interrupting," Charles stated. Annabelle pressed her forehead against his shoulder and giggled.

"Interrupt — wait a second." Beatrice eyed the couple suspiciously and Annabelle's stomach dropped. "Something *did* happen yesterday. I knew it. You said nothing happened." The last statement was directed at Annabelle.

Annabelle shuffled her feet nervously and couldn't meet her friends gaze. "I know," she apologised. "But I–I was in shock. I could hardly make sense of what had happened myself, let alone explain it to someone else."

"Really?" Charles gave her a playful pinch. "I thought it was pretty clear what we were doing." The dopey smile on his face warmed Annabelle's soul.

"Quiet, you." Beatrice pointed at Charles then turned back to Annabelle. "Well, I suppose I shall have to forgive you, since we are going to be sisters after all." She held her arms open and Annabelle flung herself into the hug.

"However," she warned. "You'd better work on keeping your hands off of each other. Or *at least* find a private room to do it in."

"A brilliant suggestion," Annabelle replied with a beaming smirk.

"May I?" Charles asked as though he were cutting into a dance. He grabbed Annabelle's hand and she was pulled from the room. She giggled uncontrollably.

"For goodness sake," Beatrice tutted good-humouredly. "Have a little self-control!"

Annabelle felt her ears warm. She flushed with embarrassment. Beatrice was hardly angry, but she still felt like a naughty school child.

They were saved any more scolding by the announcement of Mrs Daniels' arrival. The older woman's voice echoed through the house. "Annabelle? Where are you? I haven't seen you for weeks. Come and greet me."

Annabelle rolled her eyes and ran off to greet her aunt.

"Aunt Moira, it's good to see you again."

The old woman gave a brief smile. "It's nice to see you too, dear. How have you . . . what are . . . Where . . . Annabelle! Do stop bouncing up and down! You're making me dizzy."

Annabelle hadn't realised just how energetic her excitement was. "I'm sorry, Aunt. I'm just so happy."

Mrs Daniels smiled a bit more and shrugged her shoulders proudly. "I'm happy to see you, too."

Annabelle stopped bouncing. She smiled guiltily. "Yes," she stuttered. "Of course, I'm happy to see you." She paused. She really couldn't tell how her aunt was going to react. "But, you see, well. I'm happy about something else as well."

"Oh?" Mrs Daniels arched an eyebrow sceptically.

"Yes." Annabelle was losing her nerve. She had to say it now or she never would. "I have become engaged to Mr Hartley." She braced herself.

"Oh." That was all her aunt said. The woman stood quietly for a moment. Then she turned and walked away. "I have to speak to my husband." When she reached the stairs, she started to run, crying for Mr Daniels the whole way. "Colin!"

Annabelle stared after her aunt, rooted to the place where she stood in shock. She was standing in that same attitude five minutes later when Charles found her. He placed a gentle hand on her shoulder.

"Annabelle?" His voice broke her from her stasis. "What happened?" he asked gently.

Annabelle looked up into his eyes but was unable to say anything. Her mouth hung open.

Charles pressed a kiss to her forehead. "Everything will be fine," he whispered. Annabelle felt him stroke one of her curls. "I could take your mind off it all," he suggested.

Annabelle giggled as he kissed just below her ear.

"Oh!"

The pair froze.

Mrs Daniels came towards them, clapping her hands together. "There he is, the *man of the hour*." Her voice was shrill. Mr Daniels had clearly told her to be happy for Annabelle, but she didn't quite manage to sound genuine. "How lovely." She held her hand out to Charles. He kissed it and nodded his head in greeting.

"Mrs Daniels."

Annabelle couldn't control the nervous shake that trembled through her whole body.

"You *certainly* have been busy since you left Bath." Mrs Daniels barked a shrieking laugh and slapped Charles on the shoulder. "And I'll bet *you're* glad you didn't say yes to Mr Evans, aren't you?" She pinched Annabelle's cheeks sharply, and the young girl could feel her aunt's anger.

Annabelle laughed nervously.

Mrs Daniels grasped her hands tightly.

"Ow, Aunt Moira—"

"You know what we should do." Mrs Daniels completely ignored Annabelle's discomfort. "We should celebrate. In a few days, I'll take you to town. Just the two of us." The woman's voice was bordering on hysterical.

Annabelle had never her seen her aunt in such a peculiar mood, and she was scared. Hoping to calm her down, Annabelle agreed. "That would be nice."

The older woman hummed her approval. "Now," she suddenly exclaimed, making Annabelle jump. "I think I'd like a tour of my new property." She wandered off in search of a servant.

Annabelle let out a breath and leant against Charles' shoulder.

"That was ..."

"Very."

Despite her euphoric mood, Annabelle had very uncomfortable dreams that night.

She was in a gothic cathedral. The beautiful arches loomed dramatically, the great stone curved over those beneath them, making the ceiling seem incredibly high, and the apex seemed miles away, ending much farther than Annabelle could see. Mesmerising stained glass shone in the windows, the elaborate religious stories casting brightly coloured lights all over the room. It was like the saints were smiling down at her.

She was dressed in a beautiful gown, the stained glass reflections shimmering and changing its colour as she walked down the centre of the cathedral. She realised this was her wedding aisle.

Her family and friends were smiling at her, sitting on benches either side of her procession. They encouraged her and told her how beautiful and wonderful she was. Her mother told her how proud she was. Her father congratulated her. Mr Daniels told her she deserved this. Her sisters looked slightly jealous.

Hypnotic organ music filled the vast space, calling Annabelle back to her original purpose. The music echoed around the room, the notes chasing the high roof, racing to reach the top.

She knew this should be one of the happiest days of her life. Her future husband stood at the altar, facing away from her. But as he turned, Annabelle knew why she'd been feeling uneasy.

Instead of Charles Hartley, the man who stood there was Gregory Evans.

He wore an awful leer on his face, like some absurd villain in a play.

Annabelle cried out and tried to run back up the aisle, but her family and friends stopped her, pushing her towards the altar.

She cried and screamed, trying to fight her way out. Her shouts fell on deaf ears and taunted her as they echoed back to her, mocking her fear and desperation.

She could hear her name being called and she looked around frantically, searching out Charles, who she'd hoped had come to rescue her. But there was no one there.

She called out his name, hoping he would aid her, but Evans simply laughed, pointing upward to where Charles was tied up in the bell tower, quite unable to help her.

Annabelle began to cry as the tidal wave of the wedding party swept her ever closer to her doom.

Suddenly Beatrice was standing before her, an imposing figure, menacing enough to make the crowd stop pushing. Annabelle realised it was she who was calling her name as Beatrice stepped forward and roughly grabbed her by the shoulders and began to shake her, shouting for her to wake up.

CHAPTER SIXTEEN

"And it only happened recently?"

"Yes, Aunt. The day before you arrived."

"Oh. I see. "

"It was so romantic."

"I see."

"We're very happy."

"Yes, I get the picture."

Annabelle was sitting in the carriage with her aunt. As promised, Mrs Daniels was taking Annabelle into town to celebrate. The older woman had been insistent it be just the two of them. "It's not like I have any daughters of my own. This might be my only chance."

Mr Daniels had quietly taken Annabelle aside to inquire if she was happy with the idea.

"She seems set on it," Annabelle said with quiet resignation.

"Yes." Her uncle sighed. "I'm sure she will mention Mr Evans, but that doesn't mean you have to listen to what she has to say on the subject."

Her aunt hadn't taken long to broach the subject once she was alone with Annabelle.

"It's a shame you didn't go for Gregory," Mrs Daniels lamented. "I see now you were holding out for something else."

Annabelle sighed quietly. She took deep breaths and tried to ignore her aunt's attempts to start an argument. She was trying to come up with a suitable answer when she noticed they didn't seem to be taking the same route to town that she and Charles had taken on that fateful day.

"Aunt?" she began hesitantly. "You haven't been to this town before. Are you sure we're going the right way?"

"Yes, of course," the woman snapped without even looking up at her niece. "I gave the driver strict instructions."

This ended the conversation, and an uneasy silence once again filled the carriage. As they travelled for longer, going farther in the opposite direction to the town, Annabelle couldn't keep her concerns to herself.

"Aunt, I really do think we're on the wrong road," she expressed. "This isn't the route to town at all."

Mrs Daniels sighed, exasperated. "We're taking a different route, is all. I wanted to make a quick detour," she answered brusquely.

"Detour?" Annabelle questioned, confused.

"For goodness sake, Annabelle," snapped Mrs Daniels. "I'm trying to do something nice for you, will you *stop* arguing with me."

Annabelle was taken aback at her aunt's outburst and slumped in her seat, feeling ashamed. After a few minutes of silence, her aunt took pity on her and reached across to pat her knee.

"I'm sorry I was abrupt, darling. I just care about you so much. I want to make you happy."

Annabelle smiled half-heartedly. "Thank you, Aunt Moira."

"Why don't you read your book, and I'll let you know when we arrive."

Annabelle turned the book over in her hands. Twice she attempted to read, but she couldn't settle the uneasy feeling that surrounded her.

After an awkward twenty minutes of travelling in silence, Mrs Daniels announced that they had arrived.

"Eadesly Wood?" Annabelle asked.

"Yes, it's a nature walk," her aunt replied absentmindedly.

"A friend in Bath recommended it."

That statement did not help to ease Annabelle's sense of foreboding. Her aunt didn't have many friends in Bath, except for — *She wouldn't.*

"Aunt Moira?" Annabelle called apprehensively as they stepped out of the carriage and into the public beauty spot. "Why are we here?"

Mrs Daniels seemed distracted. Her eyes raked over the open area of the woods. "What, dear?" She clearly wasn't paying attention to Annabelle.

Before the young woman could pose her question a second time, a voice rang out across the clearing.

"Moira! Over here!"

Annabelle's blood ran cold. Her worst fears were realised when she saw Mrs Evans waving her arms madly at them. Worse than that, the woman's arrogant, smirking nephew stood just behind her.

"*This* is why we're here!" Annabelle furiously turned to her aunt. "*This* is doing something *nice* for me?"

"Don't be dramatic, Annabelle." Mrs Daniels chastised calmly. "I thought it would be nice for you to talk to each other about what happened."

"Aunt Moira, I don't want to speak to him ever again!" Annabelle started to storm back to the carriage, but her aunt's hand on her arm stopped her.

"You're being ridiculous. Stop being so childish. All you have to do is say sorry."

"Sorry? *Sorry!*" Annabelle was more furious than she ever had been in her life. Her anger overtook her but she was unable to express it. She flustered and spluttered as the Evanses drew nearer.

"Ho, Felicity!" Mrs Daniels waved her friend over. "You had a pleasant journey, I trust?"

"Quite," Mrs Evans replied jovially. "Though I think

Gregory is happier now that we've arrived." She linked arms with her friends. "We should leave them to chat. I'm sure they've both got a lot to say."

The women moved away, and Annabelle was left with Mr Evans. Annabelle felt nauseous at the sight of the smug grin on his face, but she tried to be polite.

"Mr Evans, I do apologise that my aunt has brought you here, but —"

"She tells me you're potentially engaged to Hartley," he announced over the top of her. "I've come to stake my claim before that happens."

Annabelle was shaking. "Stake your claim?" she repeated, in astonishment. She'd expected a passionate entreaty, not a claiming of property.

"Mr Evans, I'm sorry," she began, trying to keep her voice calm. "But I *refused* your offer. You have no *claim* to stake. You may feel inclined to repeat your offer, but I still have the right to decline. And there's no potentially about it, I'm *definitely* engaged to Mr Hartley," she stated boldly, trying not to get angry at his arrogance.

Mr Evans looked greatly taken aback by her speech and the boldness with which she made it, but this quickly turned to rage. He bellowed into the air in anger and frustration, taking Annabelle by the shoulders and forcing a kiss on her unsuspecting lips.

He moved back slightly to yell in her face. "You. Are. Mine." He was seething. "*I* asked for your hand first. I'm *owed* an acceptance. You *will* marry me."

He moved to kiss her again, but a hitherto petrified Annabelle angrily lashed out and caught his shin with her foot, managing a decent kick.

In shock and pain, he let her go.

She stumbled back from him and tried to catch her aunt's attention to say she needed help.

"I'll never marry you!" she shouted defiantly. People in the wood were starting to look at them. The two older ladies rushed back over to them.

"Annabelle, stop making such a scene," her aunt demanded. "People are staring."

"Let them," Annabelle cried. "I want everyone to hear that I will *not* marry him!" She pointed an angry finger at Mr Evans in case anyone was in doubt as to who *he* was.

"Yes, you will," Mr Evans contradicted. His voice had taken a hysterical tone.

Before she knew what was happening, Gregory had lunged forward and grabbed Annabelle around the waist. He lifted her off the ground and carried her towards his carriage. She swung her arms and legs about trying to knock at him, but to no avail. He had a tight grip on her, so tight that it knocked the breath from her, leaving her unable to shout for help.

"Aunt," she cried out pitifully.

Neither Mrs Daniels nor Mrs Evans moved. In fact, everyone in the woods seemed frozen to the ground in shock. Annabelle flailed hopelessly on Mr Evans' shoulder and was unceremoniously thrown into the carriage.

This seemed to break the spell on Mrs Evans. "Gre–Greg–Gregory?" She stepped towards him.

"It's fine," he snapped. "We'll marry in Gretna, to avoid any embarrassment with the Hartleys. Then after a year, when the scandal has died down, we'll visit. I'm sorry you'll not be able to attend the ceremony, but I'm sure you understand."

Annabelle heard him command the driver and the horses and then he climbed in the carriage with her. She made one last feeble attempt to get help from her aunt, but a terrified Annabelle could only watch with dread as Mrs Daniels faded into the distance.

Charles woke uncharacteristically late. He stretched out beneath the covers and revelled in the happiness that enveloped him. He'd now been engaged for two days, and they were the best two days of his life. He couldn't wait to see Annabelle. He just wished they were already married and could be alone.

His happy imaginings were interrupted by a piercing shriek.

"Colin! Colin!"

That was the unmistakable cry of Mrs Daniels. Charles wondered what trivial matter she'd gotten herself worked up over this time. However, he quickly dressed and followed the shrieking to see what was happening.

Mrs Daniels was in hysterics, crying for her husband, whilst — to everyone's surprise — Mrs Evans comforted her. "Colin." She threw herself into her husband's arms. "It's awful," she sobbed. "I'm so upset. Never has this happened to me before, I'll never be right again."

Mr Daniels held his weeping wife. "Whatever's happened?" he asked, confused and concerned. "Are you hurt? Why is Mrs Evans here?"

Charles turned to the new arrival. She was looking sheepish and embarrassed, staring at the floor so she didn't look anyone in the eye.

"What is going on?" Charles asked. He tried to keep his voice level and measured but to be quite frank, the sight of an Evans did not sit well with him.

"What happened?" he repeated, a little louder.

"Well — I — It — " Mrs Evans floundered.

Then Charles realized something very important. "Where's Annabelle?" he demanded, cutting Mrs Evans off mid-bluster. A nasty thought took root in his mind when the woman flushed deep red and Mrs Daniels' wailing became even more aggressive.

Charles was beginning to lose his patience. "Where is my fiancée?" He pulled Mrs Evans around to face him. Both women went quiet.

Mr Daniels, it seemed, had started to share Charles' suspicions. "Moira," he spoke gently to his wife. "What have you done?"

"He's taken her," the woman wailed into her husband's chest. "It's the worst thing that's ever happened to me in my life."

"*He?*" Charles questioned incredulously. His grip tightened on Mrs Evans. "*He* would be *your* nephew I assume. And what, pray tell, was he doing here? And where has he taken my fiancée?"

Mrs Evans floundered. Embarrassed and distressed, she couldn't bring herself to say anything. Charles sighed in exasperation and looked pleadingly at Beatrice.

"Mrs Daniels," his sister spoke softly to the sobbing woman. "Please tell us what happened to Annabelle. We have to help her."

"He's taking her to Scotland to wed," the old woman admitted in between heaving breaths. She looked up into her husband's face. "I wanted them married, but not like this." She began crying anew. Her husband released her from his embrace and looked her dead in the eye.

"Please don't tell me this is *your* doing," Mr Daniels pleaded. "That *you* brought him here." He wasn't angry. His voice was quiet and sad, resigned, as if he didn't want to believe what he heard yet knew it to be true.

His wife didn't answer, but her silence was as good as any confession. His voice belied his disappointment.

"What manner of stupidity possessed you? Were you so blinded by your — " he waved his hands vaguely at Mrs Evans trying to find the right word — "friendship with *this* woman, that you've completely disregarded your own *niece*?"

Mrs Daniels was unable to answer, her hysterical sobbing making her quite unintelligible.

"Mrs Evans?" Beatrice spoke in a calm, soothing tone — not that her serenity did anything to calm Charles. "Please would you take Mrs Daniels to the drawing room and get her some tea, she needs to be calmed. It's up the stairs, second room on the left. We" — she gestured to herself and the two men — "will discuss the situation and select a course of action."

Mrs Evans led her friend away, who wailed apologies as she left.

"It's not *us* who need an apology," her husband stated coldly. "*If* we find her," he said pointedly, "it's Annabelle who will require recompense."

In true dramatic fashion, the shame became too much, and Mrs Daniels was overcome, fainting away in the hall. She was laid on a nearby sofa to recover, Mrs Evans staying by her side to avoid any scrutiny from the others.

Charles was silent, trying to understand what was happening. He didn't want to scream and yell and scare the ladies, but he was angry and frightened. He couldn't believe Mrs Daniels had been that stupid and that deceptive. His whole body was shaking, and he looked to his sister and Mr Daniels in despair.

"We must go after them," he demanded, his voice breaking. "Straight away. Before they get too far. We've already wasted enough time. I'll take a horse. I'll be faster on my own."

Beatrice laid a hand on his shoulder. "Are you sure that's wise?" she asked gently. "We don't know where they are. You could be lost as well."

Charles tried to be appreciative of his sister's concern, but he was full of anxiety. "Well, I can't just sit here and do nothing," he snapped.

Beatrice gave him a sad smile and nodded her head. Charles watched her walk over to the two inconsolable women. They spoke, though he couldn't hear what they were saying.

He was grateful to have Beatrice. He wasn't able to stay calm right now.

"They met at Eadesly Woods about an hour ago," she informed him when she came back.

Charles made some calculations. "If he really wants to go to Scotland, he'll be going north," he conjectured. "If I cut across the fields, I may be able to intercept them at The Hart's Heart."

Beatrice wrapped him in a hug. "Please be safe."

Mr Daniels patted him on the shoulder. "Bring her back."

Charles raced to the stables, not even bothering to saddle his horse. He was off like a shot.

As he rode, he realised he didn't know what he would do when he caught up to them. *If* he caught up to them. It wouldn't be proper for him to engage in a duel, but he at least wanted to punch the man in the face.

He shuddered. He *had* to catch up with them.

He pressed his horse to go faster, the anger inside him pushing him harder. He *had* to find them . . . before it was too late.

CHAPTER SEVENTEEN

Annabelle refused to say anything. She sat in angry, defiant silence as Evans tried to engage her. She refused to acknowledge him, not even deigning to look at him.

"Come on, *cariad*," the Welshman coaxed. "You have to admit it's romantic. It's like those silly little books you read— your true love has rescued you."

"You're delusional," Annabelle spat, finally breaking her vow of silence.

Mr Evans tutted, as though he was talking to a school child. "Don't be like that, Annabelle *bach*." He put his hand under her chin to pull her gaze to his.

Annabelle snapped her head back sharply.

"I'm the hero, and you're the heroine," he continued. "We're meant to be, I know you feel it too."

Annabelle glared at him ferociously. "I thought I made *my* feelings perfectly clear on the matter when I *refused* you!"

Mr Evans bit out a laugh and raised his hand. Annabelle braced herself, sure he was going to strike her. Instead, he took a deep breath and lowered his hand again, taking her hands in his.

"I *know* what a refusal means," he told her in a rough voice. "I know that it means a girl wants the man to prove his love. Take this"—he gesticulated around him—"as my grand gesture."

"Kidnapping?" she cried incredulously. "Because that would make you the *villain* in any of the novels I've read."

As the carriage had slowed to let another pass, Annabelle

saw her chance. She leapt up from her seat and reached for the door. She had it halfway open before Mr Evans reacted. He grabbed her by the waist and pulled her onto the seat.

"Let me go," she yelled, beginning to cry. She kicked her legs at her assailant, but he just laughed.

He grabbed her wrists and pushed her into a prone position on the seat. "Don't try that again," he said in a tired voice. "This is happening, *cariad*, accept it." He loomed over her with a leering smile. "I'd rather you were willing, but I'm not afraid to use force." He momentarily tightened his grip on her wrists, then let her go.

Annabelle sat up and threw herself into the opposite corner of the carriage from Mr Evans. She curled herself up and rested her head on her knees, her body shaking violently.

"No more escape attempts, Annabelle *bach*. I don't want to have to tie you up."

With a devious laugh, Mr Evans leant back in his seat and watched her.

Annabelle's skin was crawling. She felt physically sick and her mind was reeling.

How could Aunt Moira do this? She didn't help. She just stood there and watched. Is she happy about this? Oh God, they're all deluded.

What will she tell Charles? He'll think I've run away and abandoned him. Even if he does give chase, he likely won't catch us.

She closed her eyes and tried to imagine the scenario.

There would be a shout from behind them and the carriage would roll to a stop. And the —

Don't be ridiculous, Annabelle. Nobody's going to save you, this isn't a fairy tale. You're going to have to save yourself.

She looked up to see Mr Evans grinning maniacally at her. Did he know what she was thinking? She straightened up slowly and crossed her arms over her chest.

"Where are we?" she asked as casually as she could. As she looked out of the window, she didn't recognise any landmarks.

"Never you mind that," Mr Evans commented. "I'll let you know when we get to Scotland."

She went silent. "I'm hungry," she announced moments later.

Mr Evans huffed and rolled his eyes. "How stupid do you think I am, love?" Then his stomach emitted a loud growl. "It has been a while since breakfast," he muttered under his breath. He tapped a finger against his chin pensively.

Annabelle's heart leapt. *Just stay calm,* she warned herself. "I won't try to run, I promise. I just want some food."

She watched Mr Evans mull the idea over in his mind. His eyes hardened and defeat swept through her.

And then the carriage stopped. They'd pulled into the courtyard of an inn. Peeking out of the window, Annabelle saw a sign with a small deer on it.

Mr Evans hammered on the roof. "What's going on?" he barked to the driver. The other man came around to the window.

"Sorry, sir," he mumbled. "Sorry to stop, sir, but the 'orses, they can't go no further. We must rest 'em." He was wringing his hat in his hands nervously, looking anywhere but at Annabelle.

Mr Evans swore loudly. "We can't stop!" he barked.

The driver wrung his hat tighter. "Sir, it's not possible. These 'orses, they've been pushed as far as they can go. They can't do no more."

"Dammit!"

Annabelle and the driver winced. "Fine," he said at last. "I'll get us some food."

He exited the carriage, and Annabelle started to follow him, but he slammed the door before she could descend. He waggled his finger and tutted. "You wait right here, *cariad.*"

He locked the door and put the key in his pocket. "Watch

her," he growled to the driver, then he stalked into the inn.

The minute he was gone, Annabelle desperately tried the door. She pushed and pulled with all her might but the lock wouldn't surrender.

"Help me," she called to the driver. He stood with his back to the door and he refused to look at her.

"Please."

The man half turned towards her. "I ain't got a key," he said forlornly.

She set to work with the next option open to her. She pushed the window down as far as it would go and leant out of it. She managed to get her upper body out, but she couldn't get her hips out of the opening.

Annabelle gave a frustrated cry and crawled back in. In desperation, she threw her shoe at the door. She knew it wouldn't work but she wanted to feel as though she was trying.

She sat despondently on the floor of the carriage.

"Annabelle? Annabelle Knight?"

The girl's head snapped up. She scrambled to the window and saw a familiar face.

"Mrs Lutton!"

Annabelle was so relieved she felt dizzy. "Mrs Lutton, thank goodness." She grasped at the old woman's hand.

"How are you, dear? I was so happy to hear of your engagement. Is Mr Hartley with you?" Mrs Lutton strained her neck to see into the carriage.

"No. No. Mrs Lutton, please help me. Mr Evans has locked me in."

"Mr Evans? What do you mean? George!"

General Lutton strode over to them with a concerned expression.

"Miss Knight says she's locked in. Open the door, will you?" Mrs Lutton watched anxiously as her husband furiously tried the door.

"All right," the man said at length after he'd tried the door several times. "Stand back."

Annabelle squealed and pressed herself against the other carriage door as Mr Lutton drew a pistol and pointed it at the lock. She heard a loud bang and saw a swirling cloud of smoke. When it cleared, the door was swinging open. Annabelle clambered across the carriage and into Mrs Lutton's arms. She sobbed with relief.

Unfortunately, the gunshot had drawn the occupants of the inn out into the open.

"Who the devil are *you*?" Mr Evans bellowed, angrily storming over to the carriage.

Mrs Lutton stood before Annabelle, her hands on her hips. "I might ask you the same question."

"I'm her fiancé, soon to be husband," Mr Evans sneered. "Get away from her."

"You most certainly *aren't*," General Lutton cut in.

"Yes!" Mrs Lutton shouted excitedly. She reached into her purse. "I have it on *good* authority," she announced, holding a letter aloft, "that this young lady is engaged to *another* gentleman."

By now, quite a big crowd had gathered to watch the spectacle. Annabelle heard a gasp echo amongst the assembly.

Mr Evans scoffed, though he looked nervous. "She's changed her mind," he blustered. "She's agreed to marry me, as was *originally* intended."

"I *haven't*!" Annabelle cried out, making sure as many people as possible heard her. "He's lying. He proposed to me, but I declined. I'm engaged to Mr Hartley."

Realising that he'd no rebuttal, Mr Evans roared in anger, such a frightful sound that even Mrs Lutton took a step back. "They're lying," he screamed at the crowd. His eyes darted about madly. Then, he lunged and grabbed Annabelle, pulling her away from her elderly protectors.

"We *will* be married," he bellowed. "And you won't stop us." The hysteria in his voice sent chills down Annabelle's spine.

Mr Evans seized one of the horses that was grazing near the carriage. He pushed Annabelle onto it. He ripped her dress so she could sit astride rather than side-saddle to prevent her being able to jump off as easily. It was all such a startling affair that it took several moments for the surrounding crowd to jump into action. But by then it was too late.

Evans leapt up behind her. He pulled her tight against him, then spurred the horse into a gallop.

"Why are you doing this?" Annabelle shouted above the wind rushing around them that had already ripped the bonnet from her head.

They were going so fast Annabelle's fingers were turning white as she gripped the horse's mane, trying to keep herself steady. She was also trying not to be too close to Evans. She didn't want to feel him around her. She wasn't far enough away to miss the laugh that rippled in his chest.

"You've brought this upon yourself," he growled close to her ear. "If you'd simply accepted me as you were supposed to, this wouldn't have happened. I *won't* be refused. I won't be disrespected in that way. What kind of man would I be if I didn't challenge such a dishonour made against me?" When he laughed again, Annabelle shivered.

"This will be no kind of marriage," she threatened, hoping her nerves weren't transferring into her voice. "I won't be any kind of wife to you."

Evans pushed himself forward, pressing against her. "Oh, I know that," he sneered. "It'll be no kind of affectionate marriage for you. It could have been. But now you'll have to be punished for your insolence."

He laughed viciously. "And with regards to your spousal

duties. Anything that you don't give to me, I'll take regard-less, as is my right as your husband." He took the reins in one hand, with as the other he reached up to grab at her figure over her clothes, to illustrate his point.

"You're an absolute monster," Annabelle cried out. This time fear truly coloured her voice as she struggled to pry his hand from her body. "They'll be coming after us. They will find us and stop you." Her voice broke in panic.

"I'm sure they are," he replied. "But it'll be too late. One way or another, I'll get what I want." He ran his hand down her body and along her thigh. "If I can't marry you, I'll make sure no man will ever want to."

CHAPTER EIGHTEEN

Charles rode with furious speed through the open countryside. Ahead of him, he could see the inn. The Hart's Heart. It had taken even less time than he thought, but he feared he still hadn't been quick enough.

A large group stood outside the establishment. They appeared to be in a state of frenzy. Everyone was chattering noisily, a cacophony of excited voices. Within the din, Charles heard a shout.

"Lo! Hartley!"

General Lutton walked out of the crowd. He waved an arm to flag Charles down.

Charles directed the horse toward the other man. "What news, General?" he inquired hopefully. "Has my Annabelle passed through here?"

The General nodded curtly. "You just missed her," he said sadly. Beside him, Mrs Lutton was dabbing her face with a handkerchief.

"We did our best," she sniffed dejectedly. "But I only fear we made it worse. That Welshman was terribly angry."

Charles felt his heart stop, his grip on the horse tightened. He had to be calm. His being irrational wouldn't help Annabelle.

"Which way did they go?" He was trying to be level-headed, but he knew his voice sounded panicked and shaky.

"Took a left at the crossroads," General Lutton directed. "We'll follow you with the carriage. We were just getting ready to chase after them."

Charles nodded firmly. Pulling on his horse's reins, he galloped in the direction that had been pointed out. He heard the General shout *Godspeed* after him.

He pushed his horse to go as fast as he could, the beat of its hooves adding to the deafening rush of wind as he raced to find his love.

"I'm coming Annabelle," he promised into the air.

Annabelle, at that moment, was beginning to feel very sore. To begin with, she wasn't used to riding in such a manner. In addition, in his haste to get them speedily away, Evans had forgone a saddle.

Her face stung from the wind. Sat in front of Evans and bonnet-less, she took the full brunt of its force. The wind whipped against her so hard it was like being hit with a solid object. Her hands were starting to go numb from holding on so tightly to the horse's mane.

Her heart hammered in her chest, and it wasn't just the uncomfortable ride that was making her feel sick.

If I can't marry you, I'll make sure no man will ever want to.

The words rang in her ears, and the malice behind them wrapped itself around her heart, squeezing her until she felt as though she couldn't breathe. She tried to maintain hope. She'd had it mere moments ago, only to see it cruelly ripped away as Evans tore her from her friend. She would have cried if the cold air hadn't frozen her face.

They'd been galloping at full force ever since they'd left the inn. Annabelle's stomach lurched when Evans suddenly, joltingly, slowed his pace. Her heart faltered when she saw a church steeple peeking out through the trees.

"A parish," the Welshman cried gleefully. "Sorry, my dear," he said as he urged the horse on towards a small local church. "It seems we won't be wed in Scotland after all. I'm sorry you won't get a wedding dress. Although, I suppose it's best you don't start this marriage with any misconceptions of wealth, comfort, or respect for your wishes." He laughed again, and Annabelle's spirit truly broke.

They approached the rector's cottage, the church just behind it, and Evans dismounted. He pulled Annabelle down roughly after him. His grip was painfully tight on Annabelle's arm. He banged ferociously on the door. "Open up," he shouted.

Eventually, the door was opened by a very grumpy-looking man. "Can I help you?" he asked indignantly, clearly annoyed at being disturbed from whatever he'd been doing.

"We need to be married immediately," Evans demanded.

The vicar looked between Gregory and Annabelle. "That's not possible," he declined. "There's a considerable amount of paperwork to be done. I must have consent from the young lady's parents or guardians—"

His speech was cut short as Evans reached into his waistband to bring out his military issue pistol. "I hope you understand the urgency of my request." Evans waved the weapon in front of the clergyman.

The religious man gulped nervously.

"I'll fetch the registry," he stuttered, running back into the house.

"You're a cruel man," Annabelle cried to Evans, as the man drew away. "I'll never love you or respect you."

"That doesn't wound my soul as much as you think it does," he sneered. His smile dropped quickly at an unexpected noise coming from the main road. Annabelle couldn't see anything from where she was, but she could hear without issue.

A horse whinnied, its hooves beating on the ground. The rider's voice soon rang out, filled with concern and desperation.

"Annabelle?"

"Charles!" Annabelle cried in disbelief. She still couldn't see him, so she cried out again, hoping to give away their location. "Charl —" Her second shout was cut short when Evans clamped his hand over her mouth and pulled her into the vicar's home.

"Take us to the church," he demanded wildly. He waved the gun in a threatening manner but was forced to put it away when Annabelle began to fight him.

Charles appeared at the top of the path and Annabelle's heart lifted. But it dropped again when Evans levelled his pistol at the horse and his rider.

Annabelle fought him with all her might and was able to change Evans' stance enough that he missed when he pulled the trigger. Nevertheless, the horse was spooked and reared up, throwing Charles to the ground.

Annabelle cried out as Evans forwent trying to shoot him again and just hauled her along to the church.

To Annabelle, the picturesque appearance of the place seemed contradictory to the foul actions that would be happening very soon within those walls. She hated the idea of being married to Evans whilst being watched by the saints and angels who graced the stained-glass windows.

As they approached, she heard choral singing from inside the medieval structure.

The vicar looked nervously at the pistol and then to Evans. "It would seem the ladies' choir is rehearsing," he stammered, clutching his bible.

Evans pushed him aside to barge through the heavy wooden doors. "I'm afraid I'm going to have to cut your meeting short, ladies," he announced to the singers viciously. They looked at him, but none moved. He brought his pistol to their attention, firing once into the air above their heads. "Now!" he barked. The ladies shrieked and ran from the church.

Evans returned to Annabelle and the vicar. "I think you'll

find the church is now available for our use," he stated wickedly. He pulled Annabelle by the arm and motioned for the vicar to go first. He forced the party to the altar. "Begin," he instructed, levelling the pistol at the vicar.

The vicar coughed nervously and opened his Bible. "What will you do about the matter of witnesses?" he asked cautiously. Evans gave him a stern look and shot once more into the air.

"We'll be fine without," the clergyman conceded, his eyes still on the smoking gun. He looked up at Annabelle. She was clearly frightened, a flood of tears rolling down her face.

She looked back at him pleadingly, scared of what Evans would do if she spoke up.

The vicar swallowed and took a deep breath. He snapped his Bible shut. "I can't do it," he said, obviously trying to sound strong and powerful, but his voice wavered slightly. "Shoot me if you must, but I can't."

Evans growled viciously. "Marry us now or suffer the consequences," he threatened. He pushed the muzzle of the gun against the vicar's robes. But the man of God stood stoically tall, no doubt praying he'd have the strength to stand his ground in the face of death. He was, in fact, spared that effort.

"Evans!" Charles' voice boomed across the church. "Move away from her, you scoundrel," he ordered as he advanced the length of the church.

"Charles!" Annabelle cried in relief. She tried to run to him, but Evans seized her. He pulled her from the altar, towards the stairway that led up to the tower.

"She's mine!" he shouted to Charles as he forced her up the stairs. He kicked a door open and threw Annabelle to the ground. By her guess, she was in an unoccupied study. Oak furniture filled the room, along with a large number of books.

Annabelle screamed with all the power of her lungs. Mr Evans propped a chair against the door, barricading them in.

Then he turned to her and rubbed his hands together eagerly.

"We may not be married," he said darkly. "But Hartley won't want you after this." He loomed over Annabelle like a monster.

Knowing she wasn't alone returned the fire to Annabelle's spirit. She took the remaining shoe from her foot and launched it at her attacker, catching him just above his right ear. Then, she scrambled to her feet and launched herself across the room.

"You won't get away with this," she shouted determinedly. She swung her fists and hit any part of Mr Evans that she could. "You. Won't. Win!" Every word was punctuated with a blow, but the man seemed unbothered.

He laughed dryly. "I already have," he gloated.

"No!" Annabelle cried out in fury and made one last attempt with the remains of her energy to pass him and get out. Her hand was inches from the door handle when Evans grabbed her by the hair and pulled her backwards.

The door began to shake, and soon it was pushed open, sending the chair flying across the room.

That was the moment when Charles made his entrance. He ran towards the couple and grabbed Evans by the shoulders and hurled him across the room.

Annabelle reached out for him, crying with relief. But as he bent down to help Annabelle up, Charles was tackled by his rival. Annabelle shrieked as she watched his head strike the floor.

Madly reaching around her, Annabelle picked up the first thing that came to hand. She sent a book sailing towards Evans as he neared her again. The man stumbled back, dazed. Annabelle flew to Charles' side.

He looked up at her, slightly disoriented, but he seemed to care little for his own wellbeing.

"Are you unharmed?" He reached up to her face.

"Not for long," Evans fumed. He grabbed Charles by the lapel and tossed him aside. With his other hand, he pressed Annabelle against the bookcase.

"Where were we?" he leered. His eyes flashed madly Annabelle was sure he had broken, he was completely insane.

She squeezed her eyes shut. She reached deep within herself to find some energy.

"Don't touch her, you villain," Charles growled from across the room with more anger in his voice than Annabelle had ever heard.

The next moment, wood shattered in every direction. Evans groaned in pain, and he and Annabelle fell to the floor.

Charles stood over them breathing heavily, the back half of an old chair still in his hands.

Annabelle surveyed the scene, weary and exhausted. Evans was in a still heap across her legs.

"Help me with him," she asked. Her voice didn't sound at all familiar. She almost felt as if as if she was hearing another person say speak her words.

Charles hauled Evans off her and laid him against a table that had been upended in the fight. He wasn't moving.

"Is he dead?" Her voice was shaky. She didn't know which answer she wanted.

"Just unconscious," Charles told her softly.

"What do we do?"

"Make sure he can't leave."

Annabelle couldn't help but laugh as Charles' eyes widened when she pulled off her stockings. "I can't see anything else to secure him with."

Charles finished the deed and wrapped Annabelle in his arms as they heard men entering the church.

The gravity of what had happened to her—and what had almost happened—struck home. She began to sob uncontrollably as a pair of strong arms wrapped around her, enveloping her in a protective shield.

She felt the energy leave her body, passing through her toes into the wooden floor beneath her feet. The strong arms help her up, cradling her. She let herself drift away.

CHAPTER NINETEEN

Charles caught Annabelle as she collapsed in his arms. He brought them both gently to the floor and held her against him. He murmured softly to her and stroked her hair, quite incapable of doing anything else.

He heard footsteps thunder up the staircase.

"Hartley?" He recognized General Lutton's deep baritone.

"In here." Charles tried not to shout too loudly. He didn't want to wake Annabelle.

The General joined him moments later with what appeared to be a band of men. Charles watched him take in the scene in the room. He couldn't help but laugh when Lutton shrugged his shoulders and began barking orders to the men behind him.

"Secure him. Make sure he can't escape. Check that the vicar has sent for the magistrate."

The man then laid a gentle hand on Charles' shoulder.

"Do you want me to take her?"

Charles gripped Annabelle tighter. He wasn't ever going to let her go. "No," he said shortly.

Lutton chuckled. "Fine. But at least take her out of here. I don't want her to be around when that blackguard wakes up."

Charles cast his glance toward Evans. Rage boiled inside him, but when Annabelle shifted against him in her sleep, he calmed himself.

He scooped his fiancée up in his arms and held her close. Carefully, he made his way out of the room and down the stairs, into the main area of the church. When he descended, he saw the vicar kneeling at the altar. He could hear the quiet whispers of prayers.

Slowly, he went over to the man and manoeuvred until he was sat down next to him, Annabelle nestled in his lap.

"I heard what you said." He addressed the vicar when he was sure the other man had finished his prayer. "What you were prepared to do for her."

He tried to remain level, but he couldn't stop the sobs that erupted from his chest. The clergyman laid a consoling hand on his shoulder.

"I'm glad I could help." Then he left Charles sitting at the altar.

Charles looked down at the sleeping girl in his arms, and gently brushed a curl from her face. Looking at her, he couldn't believe he'd nearly lost her today. His heart panged at the thought of it and he knew, as he looked at her, he'd made the right decision asking her to marry him. He didn't want to spend another moment without her.

Annabelle's eyelids fluttered, and quickly her eyes were searching his, piercing deep within him. He leaned forward and placed a delicate kiss on her forehead. He lingered there, their faces barely touching, both of them simply revelling in being close and being together. Annabelle was clearly fighting the strength of her eyelids.

Kissing her again, Charles whispered gently to her. "Rest my love, we'll return to Godshollow soon." He cradled her as she rested against him.

Soon, General Lutton joined him. The man was straightening his coat and his cuffs. He gave Charles a nod.

"That man's not going anywhere," he said plainly. "The magistrate will deal with him when he gets here. It's all over. Let's get you two safely home."

"Thank you." Charles' voice cracked with emotion.

Slowly, he stood and followed the General from the church. In the churchyard, they found Mrs Lutton anxiously pacing.

"There you are!" she cried happily. On seeing the dozing Annabelle, she apologised and dropped the volume of her voice. "Is she well? What happened? Where is he?"

"All in good time, dear," General Lutton told her as he helped Charles and Annabelle into the carriage. Charles sat Annabelle in the corner, gently resting her head on his shoulder.

Mrs Lutton scrambled in behind them. "For goodness sake, dear boy," she admonished him. "Don't be modest. Don't move on our account, comfort your fiancée. We're not so prudish as to be perturbed by some physical consolation between lovers."

Gratefully, Charles thanked her and gently manoeuvred Annabelle onto his lap.

A few moments later, General Lutton joined them.

"I've given your address to the vicar. The magistrate may want to speak to you, but I think you just want to be at home now."

Charles nodded tiredly.

The carriage moved away. As they travelled to Godshollow, Charles told them what he could of the ordeal.

"And he was really determined to marry her, no matter what?" Mrs Lutton asked, bewildered.

"Not in the end," Charles admitted slowly. "I think he just wanted to humiliate her and get back at me for *stealing* her."

"Oh!" cried Mrs Lutton. "Such villainy! I'd never wish to believe a man capable of such, particularly against such a lovely girl. I do hope he'll feel the full force of the law." She paused briefly. "If not . . . I may have to see to him myself. Just despicable." The old woman gripped her cane and gave it a shake, clearly thinking of what she would like to do to Evans.

Once again Charles found himself unable not to laugh at the woman's spirit, grateful of her devoted friendship. He was also considering that being *seen to* by Mrs Lutton would be a far worse fate than anything the law could devise for the man.

"But how did he know she was here?" the General asked perplexed.

Annabelle stirred in Charles' arms. "Aunt Moira," she murmured sleepily.

"She and the fiend's aunt are friends," Charles explained. "She joined us from Bath a few days ago. She must have told the Evanses to come with her."

"So angry I said no." Annabelle began to sit up a bit straighter and rubbed her eyes, but she didn't move from Charles' embrace.

Mrs Lutton reached across and laid a hand on Annabelle's arm. "Well, you're safe now, dear." She smiled apologetically. "I was so worried I'd made things worse. I dread to think what's happened to you since we were separated."

"Thank you for trying to help at all," Annabelle said quietly. "I was losing my faith in a rescue. I do hope neither of you were hurt."

"Not a scratch," General Lutton assured her.

Annabelle let out a relieved sigh, and Charles felt her go limp in his arms again. He was having to fight his own eyelids to stay awake.

"Sleep," Mrs Lutton ordered. "We'll wake you when you're home."

Charles almost immediately gave in to the drowsiness that encompassed him. He was finally able to relax.

"Mr Hartley?"

"Son, wake up."

Charles was roused by the Luttons and realised they must

have arrived at Godshollow. He gently woke Annabelle and helped her from the carriage. An arm around her waist, he helped her inside.

They were immediately met by Beatrice and Mr Daniels.

"Thank goodness!" cried the former, rushing to envelope the couple in a hug. "We've been so worried." Releasing them from her bone-crushing hug, she stepped aside so Mr Daniels could share in the happiness.

The old man embraced his niece, apologising to her over and over. Then he pulled Charles into a tight hug. "Thank you," he whispered emotionally.

Charles felt Annabelle stiffen and looked down at her. She was searching the room.

"Where's my aunt?" she asked in a quiet voice.

Mr Daniels sighed despondently. "She's not here. I was so ashamed by what she'd done I told her not to be here when you got back."

Annabelle nodded slowly and began to cry. She rushed into her uncle's arms.

"I'm so sorry," he whispered repeatedly, shedding tears himself.

A clock in the hall chimed loudly, informing everyone of the lateness of the hour. But when Charles looked at the others, he saw that none of them wanted to go to bed right now. Mr Daniels was watching his niece as if he was afraid she'd vanish in front of his eyes.

"You've had a long day," Daniels said with a shaky voice. "You must be hungry. I'll get some food sent up to the parlour."

The four of them, followed by General and Mrs Lutton, went to await the food after Daniels had sent a boy off with the instructions.

Charles sat on the sofa with his arm around Annabelle, not wanting to let her go.

The room was silent for a long moment.

Then Mr Daniels gazed at his niece and began to cry again. He was apologising as he was sobbing. He clearly saw this as his fault because of his wife.

Charles was going to say something to him, but General Lutton led Daniels out of the room. The ex-army man could probably do a lot better at consoling his brother-in-arms than he could.

Not long after, Mrs Lutton excused herself as well, and the three young people were left on their own.

Charles glanced down at Annabelle and saw that she'd fallen asleep again.

"Where's Jasper?" Charles asked as he finally noticed his brother's absence.

"He went to fetch a magistrate," Beatrice replied. "He left not long after you did. When he returned, he said that the lawman would be with us in the morning, and then he went to bed."

Charles nodded. Despite Jasper's lack of outward emotion, he was calm under pressure. His unaffected air was actually comforting in times like these, his way of showing affection.

A clock chimed again and informed the house that they were into the next day.

Charles gently shook Annabelle. "Why don't you go to bed?" he asked quietly.

Her eyes were fearful at his suggestion. "I don't want to be alone," she answered quickly.

"Then we will all sleep in here," Beatrice said.

Charles raised an eyebrow at his sister's suggestion.

"Well, I can very well guess that neither of you will want to be without the other. I will stay as a chaperone." Beatrice winked, and Charles was glad for her lightening mood.

"Annabelle, you have that sofa. Charles, you can take the floor because you're the *gentleman*. And I will curl up in this armchair. I'll ask a servant to find some blankets."

She turned back to Charles when she reached the door. "Nothing inappropriate," she warned with a smirk, pointing her finger between the couple, who were still on the sofa. "I will *not* have my reputation as a chaperone tarnished."

When she left, Charles pressed a kiss to the top of Annabelle's head. Then he put a hand under her chin and tipped her face towards his. "I'm so glad to have you safe. I don't know what I would've done if I'd lost you."

Annabelle cuddled into him and cried softly. Charles soothed her as best he could and murmured reassurances to her.

"It's okay. You're safe. He can't hurt you."

Eventually, he heard the tears end and her breathing even out, telling him she'd fallen asleep again.

He leaned his head back against the top of the sofa and closed his eyes.

He wasn't sure exactly when Beatrice had come back in, but when he opened his eyes briefly, he saw that he and Annabelle had been covered with a blanket and his sister was wrapped in another in the armchair.

He smiled. Everything was going to be all right. He drifted back off to sleep.

CHAPTER TWENTY

A nnabelle slowly woke from her slumber. She blinked several times and was confused when she wasn't in her own room. She also wasn't in a bed — she was lying on something much more solid. She lifted her head and was met with a bright smile.

"Good morning."

"Good morning."

With the drowsiness of sleep drifting away, Annabelle was able to understand where she was and why. She glanced to the chairs opposite and saw Beatrice, fast asleep and snoring lightly.

It was such a normal scene Annabelle was shocked. At various points the day before, she'd worried she would never see the Hartleys again and never have such a gloriously mundane scene greet her when she opened her eyes.

Overwhelmed, she broke down in tears. Charles hugged her closer and consoled her.

"I'm so glad to have you here," he whispered. Annabelle watched him glance over at his sister and then press an emotion-filled kiss against her lips. Annabelle relished the tingle that ran through her whole body, fully waking her. "Thank you for saving me," she said against his lips.

She felt Charles' chuckle move through his body. "By the time I got to the tower, you seemed to have everything pretty much in hand. I just offered a little extra assistance."

Annabelle playfully tapped him on the shoulder. "Well then, thank you for coming to get me."

Charles smiled at her. "I had no choice. I will always come for you, Annabelle. Not to mention, I could *not* abandon you to a man who has never read a novel."

In response, Annabelle cuddled against him more and kissed him again.

"*Excuse* me, you two, I thought I said nothing inappropriate."

With a jump, Annabelle pulled back from the kiss. From the blush on Charles' face, he hadn't realised she was awake either. He coughed self-consciously.

"Good morning, Beatrice."

"Good morning indeed," she replied with a warm smile.

Then Annabelle's stomach growled ferociously. "I didn't get to eat anything yesterday," she explained embarrassedly. It was then that the group were reminded of the food that Mr Daniels had sent for the night before.

"Then breakfast is definitely in order," Charles replied.

Beatrice led the way to the dining room, where the group found Mr Daniels.

When he saw her, her uncle wrapped Annabelle in a tight hug, inadvertently breaking the hold Charles had on her hand.

"How are you?" he asked sincerely.

Annabelle paused. Such a lot had happened that she hadn't had time to realise the reality of it. "I don't know," she replied honestly. "I'm thankful to be safe and I'm glad the ordeal is over. But I honestly don't know how to feel. I can't believe any of it happened—it all feels like a terrible dream."

Her uncle smiled at her. "That is to be expected. It was a ghastly thing to have happen to you, but try and be reassured that you're safe and well. I know *we* all are. Speaking of which, the Luttons are talking with the magistrate at the moment. But I'm sure they will be very glad to see you."

Anxiety coursed through Annabelle at the thought of

having to speak with the magistrate. She felt a reassuring squeeze on her shoulder.

"We'll do it together," Charles whispered.

Annabelle nodded and twisted a lock of her hair between her fingers.

"Have a seat, dear," Mr Daniels said gently. "You'll feel better after some food."

She sat close to the fire, and Charles placed himself next to her. She found it incredibly reassuring to have him close. Either Beatrice or Mr Daniels was always in the room, but they never mentioned the couple's behaviour, which Annabelle was grateful for.

On the table next to the sofa, Annabelle saw a note with her name on it.

"What's that?" she asked, reaching for it.

Mr Daniels snatched it up from the table looking nervous. "I suspect it's from Moira," he said slowly. "Before she left last night, she did ask for a quill and ink. You don't have to read it."

Annabelle considered it. "Where exactly has my aunt gone?"

"The Evanses are the only friends left to her now. She has gone to stay with them."

"Oh, Uncle. You must be terribly sad. I'm so sorry."

"Not a word of it," Mr Daniels said quickly. "You did nothing wrong. Moira made her own choices. I just wish she had chosen smarter."

Annabelle twisted her hands together in her lap.

"I think I want to read it," she said at length.

Hesitantly, her uncle handed it over.

Annabelle could feel Charles watching over her shoulder as, under everybody's apprehensive gaze, she read.

Dearest Annabelle,

I know that you'll find it in your heart to forgive me for what has come to pass. I'm sorry that it happened this way, but you must understand that I'm not at fault.

I was appalled by Gregory's behaviour, but it was hardly within my power to see this aspect of his personality any earlier. I don't know if Gregory's actions were part of his normal personality. I'm sure he was only driven to it by the circumstances and desperation to be with you.

You know how much a union between the two of you would've meant to me, and to his family, and I was determined to see it through. I see now that this won't be possible.

I'm sure over time, all involved will be able to forgive each other for what has occurred, as we all had some role to play in this drama.

Please don't let this harden your heart. I'll wait for your reply.

All my love,

Your dearest — and only — aunt,

Moira Daniels

Surprising herself—and those around the table—Annabelle began to laugh. She should've been angry at her aunt for refusing to take any responsibility, and to even have the audacity to go so far as to place blame on her. But all she could do was laugh. She realised that this was as close to an apology and understanding of the situation she would ever receive from the strange woman.

She then passed the letter to her bewildered companions. She watched Beatrice put a consoling hand on Mr Daniels' shoulder as they read it.

"I can only express sorrow and embarrassment over my wife's behaviour," Mr Daniels said at last.

"Nobody is blaming you," Charles told him.

"Exactly," Annabelle agreed. "Please don't feel guilty, Uncle."

Mr Daniels' expression belied his uncertainty, and he looked as though he was about to argue, but the group were soon interrupted by the Lutton's, who had finished with the magistrate.

They greeted Annabelle and Charles warmly.

"I'm so happy to see you," Mrs Lutton expressed. "Don't worry, the magistrate is lovely. Soft as a kitten."

Annabelle laughed, but she still felt nervous. Even holding Charles' hand did nothing to expel the jitters that plagued her when they were called in to speak with the lawman.

Mr Daniels insisted that he be there, so Annabelle was sat in the middle between her uncle and Charles. It fortified her to have their support, but also made her anxious about explaining everything that had happened.

The magistrate sat in a study in the east wing, and he seemed imposing and cold behind a great oak desk. But Mrs Lutton had been right. He was kind and gentle and understanding.

"Take your time," he told Annabelle. "If you're upset, we can stop."

"I just want it to be over," she answered.

She told him the whole ordeal, from its beginnings in Bath up to Charles' rescue of her the night before. She tried to stay strong, but she couldn't stop the tears as she recounted certain events. Charles had to step in to help towards the end whilst Mr Daniels hugged her.

"And neither of you received any threatening missives from the man?"

The couple both shook their heads, then Annabelle felt she needed to clarify.

"There were letters from his family that arrived. But they seemed to suggest that the whole thing was being put to an end. His cousins told me they forgave me, so I thought he had given up."

"All right. It would be helpful if I could see those letters." The magistrate straightened his papers and rose. "Thank you for talking with me. I'll be in touch soon once I have spoken properly with his lawyer.

"What will happen to him?" Annabelle asked as he was

leaving.

The man considered for a moment. "Well, he's been arrested. He'll be tried, though no court in the land would find him innocent. He could go to jail. But, most likely, given his military service, he'd be deported to the colonies."

"Australia?" Charles responded.

"Possibly. I'll make sure that you are informed of the result."

The lawman left and Mr Daniels wrapped his niece in a hug. "You're so incredibly brave, Annabelle." Then, to their surprise, he hugged Charles as well. "Thank you for bringing her home."

The rest of the day was quiet and restful. After the shock of the day before, nobody wanted to do anything too taxing. The Luttons left after lunch, needing to return home.

Annabelle took a walk around the grounds with Charles and Beatrice, then the latter took her aside to talk about wedding plans.

"I thought it might be fun to think up some ideas."

Beatrice was clearly trying her best to comfort her.

"That would be wonderful," Annabelle replied with a smile. "But what flowers will we be able to find in mid-winter?"

"I'm sure we will be able to find something to work with."

"I can't believe this is really happening," Annabelle commented as the girls were planning the wedding breakfast. "I have adored Charles since I met him at the ball, but I could only dream of marrying him, never actually doing it. I'm ever so happy, but I'm nervous as well."

"I think everyone gets nervous before a wedding," Beatrice offered. "But I will tell you one thing, I'm so glad that I'm gaining you as a sister."

The two girls hugged and went back to their planning.

At about a quarter past six, Mr Daniels called them to join the others in the dining room.

First, he informed Annabelle that her parents would be arriving in a week's time, and Major Hartley told his brother that a licence was being procured so that he and Annabelle could marry within the fortnight.

Annabelle was touched by the Major's gesture. *I think that is the most emotional thing I have ever seen him do.* It was also, quite possibly the most emotional thing Charles had ever seen him do, as the young man had tears in his eyes and offered a handshake to his brother.

That night at dinner, as Annabelle ate, she saw her uncle behaving very oddly. He was distracted and energetic. He hardly touched his food and seemed to be anxious for the dinner to be over.

Finally, when the last plates were cleared away, Mr Daniels got to his feet.

"Right, I have an announcement" — Major Hartley coughed — "Sorry, *we* have an announcement. As you know, I inherited Godshollow quite out of the blue. It's a lovely property, and I have had a wonderful time here, but I feel well settled and well suited at my home in Oxfordshire."

Annabelle had a sinking feeling in her stomach. *Please don't say he is selling Godshollow!*

"When I first decided to visit," he continued, "the plan was that we'd sell it. But, as I feared, having seen it, I've fallen in love with the property and don't want to part with it. On the other hand, I don't want to leave my home." He paused like a circus ringleader baiting a crowd. "So, I've decided," he declared dramatically, "that Major Hartley is going to run the estate for me."

A gasp spread across the room like ripples on a lake.

"He knows the area well," Mr Daniels continued, pleased by everyone's reactions. "And, I don't mean to be rude" — he looked to Charles and Beatrice — "but I'm aware of the difficultly you've been having since the death of your father.

"I will, of course, still be owner, and Major and Miss Hartley shall be tenants. But it'll effectively be their home. Though my family will be allowed to visit whenever we choose," he explained with a wink.

"It's the best of both worlds. I don't have to give up the property, but I also don't have to move. I've gained an excellent estate manager, and the Hartleys get to return to their home county."

Everyone was at a loss for words. They weren't shocked in a bad way, but every mouth was open, except for Beatrice, who had begun to cry.

"I don't know how to thank you," Charles began with an arm around his sister. "You can see how much this means."

Mr Daniels smiled. "There's no need of thanks. It's an effective business solution which happens to make every party happy—a rare thing, I can tell you."

There was a lot of celebrating to be done that night. Toasts were made for the upcoming wedding, for Annabelle's safety, and for the Hartleys managing Godshollow. And everybody went to bed with lighter hearts than they'd had the previous day.

Chapter Twenty-One

Charles and Annabelle were married twelve days later. Her parents joined them at Godshollow six days before the ceremony. They were overjoyed to see their daughter, and they bombarded her with hugs and kisses the moment she greeted them in the foyer.

Mr Daniels had written to them about what had happened — he showed Annabelle the letter before sending it — and while he had assured them everything was all right now, they were still anxious when they saw their daughter.

"You poor child," her mother wailed as she hugged her. "I never did like Moira. I'm sorry, Colin, but there was always something about her."

Her father was slightly less frantic, but still held her longer than he usually did, and he whispered to her how proud he was.

When Annabelle introduced Charles, her mother had kissed his cheek and her father had shaken his hand, whilst expressing his gratitude for everything he had done.

But, no sooner had everyone been introduced than Mrs Knight had started planning for the wedding, shutting herself, Annabelle, and Beatrice in a room, arguing that men couldn't plan a celebration properly.

The next day, the women went out to the nearest town — two hours away, it was hardly nearby, but close enough for a day trip.

There they placed an order for Annabelle's wedding dress which they were assured would be ready in time for the wedding, thanks to a capable team of seamstresses. According to the proprietress, she and her ladies were as fast as the top seamstresses in London.

The dress did, in fact, arrive the day before the wedding, and when Annabelle tried it on, she nearly cried.

They had measured her perfectly. The satin gown fell gracefully over her curves and poured to the floor, giving her the perfect column figure. The bodice crossed her chest, making a tasteful *V*. A deeper blue than she remembered, the colour made her gown shine without washing her out, the silver adding shimmering threads of relief from the dark block, the elegant band under her bust breaking it up.

As she beheld herself in the mirror, she couldn't have been happier with what she saw.

The night before the wedding, Annabelle's mother came to her when everyone had gone to bed.

She sat in front of her daughter, a box on her lap. Annabelle waited patiently.

"Annabelle, my dear. I have come to talk to you about the final act to consecrate a marriage. But before I start, I would like to tell you that there is no need to be embarrassed. I have gone through this with your sisters before now, and it's a natural thing." Annabelle nodded, sitting patiently.

Her mother seemed taken aback by her daughter's composure. "You know what it is I wish to talk to you about?" she questioned with astonishment. "I hope Mr Hartley has acted his part as a gentleman and not done anything untoward."

Annabelle nodded. "Mr Hartley has been the perfect gentleman," she assured her mother.

"Of course." Mrs Knight seemed to calm her panic. "But I have to say your sisters were not nearly so composed as you are."

Annabelle twisted her hands in her lap. "Well, my sisters

did mention something about making a marriage official, though they never told me what it was. And, whenever they asked me, they told me to read Fanny Sparrow." Whilst she wasn't sure if the author had included the specific act itself, Annabelle was sure there wasn't too much that had been left out.

She was quite mistaken.

Mrs Knight picked up a nearby book. "Let's see what she has to say."

At first, Annabelle watched her squint trying to find the right section. She finished the passage and put the book down.

"Well," her mother said with a laugh. "I think your sisters were playing with you. Miss Sparrow certainly does go into very . . . creative detail, but she hasn't mentioned anything explicit."

Annabelle panicked. She thought that she was well prepared for her wifely duties, but the books she'd read didn't come close, apparently.

"Can it go wrong?" she asked anxiously. "What if I am a poor partner?"

Her mother sighed gently and patted her daughter's knee. "If you follow your husband's lead, there's little that you *can* do wrong. The man takes the lead in these matters, you simply follow him, he won't lead you astray."

Annabelle was slightly reassured, but she was still mortified at what she had thought was her cultured understanding of how things went between a wife and husband.

"I know you will do well," her mother stated kindly, "in this and all other wifely duties." She took the box in her hands and stood up from her seat. She hovered in the doorway.

"It's always hard to give up a child," she muttered, her voice sounding on the verge of tears. "But I'm sure that I'm giving you to the best possible man. You've done well my dear, I know you will be happy." She held out her arms to embrace her daughter, who put her arms around her mother and held her tight.

"Thank you, Mother," she whispered against her. "For the lessons, for everything. I will miss you, but we will all visit very often. I thank you for the life you've given me thus far, and I am excited to be starting a new one with Mr Hartley."

Mother and daughter hugged each other close.

The wedding was being held in the church that was part of Charles' living at Falton Bay. Another man conducted the ceremony, of course, but it meant a lot to him to be married there.

He stood at the altar anxiously waiting for Annabelle to enter.

It was a cold day, the sky was grey and cloudy. Not brilliant wedding weather, but when Charles beheld his bride, his whole life grew in colour and brightness.

She looked beautiful, in a long blue dress and a beaming smile that decorated her face.

When she reached him, it took all of his willpower not to reach out to her and kiss her. But he had to follow the weddings rituals. He could kiss her as much as he wanted once they were husband and wife and in his — *their* — home.

Afterwards, everyone told the happy couple how much they had enjoyed the ceremony.

"The vows and the chosen readings were wonderful. Not too short, not too long and perfectly suited to you both," Beatrice had remarked.

Charles and his new wife exited the church under a hail of rice as they made their way to their carriage, leading the group to return to Falton Bay Rectory for breakfast and celebrations.

"You have a wonderful home," his new mother-in-law

remarked kindly. "Though, it does lack a woman's touch. I'm sure once we bring Annabelle's possessions, it will be much better."

It was late in the evening by the time the couple were finally on their own.

As soon as they were alone, Charles enveloped his wife in a tight embrace. "I am so glad that I will now be able to kiss you whenever I choose." He placed one such kiss on her jawbone.

"I will admit," he mumbled against her skin. "I am grateful for the festivities and our friends' happiness for us, but, rather selfishly, I've found myself quite desperate to have you all to myself."

Annabelle giggled coyly then pulled him in for a kiss before saying, "I was thinking exactly the same thing."

Charles bent down, swooping Annabelle into his arms. He began to mount the stairs to his bedroom.

He gazed down at the beautiful woman he was carrying, and his heart felt full.

He kicked the bedroom door open with his foot and carefully set her down on the bed.

She was looking at him with love and affection, but a hint of nervousness lurked in her blue eyes.

He lifted her hand to his mouth and kissed it. "We can wait, if you aren't ready," he told her softly, although he rather hoped she didn't want to.

Then his wonderful wife, his amazing, brave, strong wife, took their clasped hands and held his cheek.

"I think, Mr Hartley, it's time for us to make our wedding official."

Chapter Twenty-two

A month after her marriage to Charles, Annabelle received a letter. It was brought to her by a maid, who said it had been forwarded from Godshollow. The missive was addressed using her maiden name. She turned it over curiously, but the seal didn't give any help to identify the author. Slowly, she opened it.

Dearest Annabelle,

I do not suppose you would wish to hear from me, but I felt I had to reach out to you.

I cannot fully express the horror I felt when I learnt of Gregory's actions or the joy I had on hearing you were safe.

I had desperately wanted us to be cousins, but you are too sweet a girl to be tied to Gregory, and I am glad that his plan failed. But I'm sure you care little as to my feelings on the matter.

Anyway, I'm writing to let you know what has happened to Gregory. I am pleased to say that he has been convicted and has been transported. He is to serve for ten years with the East India Company and it is doubtful that he will ever return.

It might also interest you to know that Carys has also departed. She met an old general when we were visiting Gregory at the militia camp before he left, and she married him the moment she knew of his large fortune. Her hopes, I suppose, were that he would die quickly, either in war or of old age. Fortunately, it seems he has immense luck on the battlefield and the constitution of an ox.

I never thought I would love anyone as much as I did my twin sister, but now I can only feel resentment that we share as much as we do. I must confess that it was Carys that set such despicable actions into Gregory's head, and I have never been more ashamed.

As I said, I had looked forward immensely to our being related but now I fear I may not even get to call you a friend any longer.

I'm sorry, Annabelle, and I hope that you have happiness in your future.

Yours,

Miss Gwenneth Evans.

Annabelle regarded the note a few times. She had liked Gwen and had always expected she was nicer than her family allowed her to be. She hadn't considered how much Gregory's actions would have affected his cousin. She knew Gwen had always spoken highly of him, so it must have been hard for her to learn he'd been so despicable.

After careful consideration, she wrote a letter back — Gwen hadn't given up all hope and had left her address on the back page. She informed Gwen that she was well and expressed her gratitude for her thoughts. Impulsively, she offered an invitation for her to visit her and her husband at Godshollow.

Speaking of whom, Annabelle went to find Charles in his study. She showed him the letter and her response.

"It's kind of her to think of you," he said at length. He had been studying the missive with an unreadable look on his face.

"Do you agree with my inviting her here?"

"As long as she is on her own."

"I'm sure she will be." She paused and worried the carpet with her foot. "I don't suppose my uncle has mentioned if Aunt Moira had sent anything?"

Charles put the papers down on his desk and stood, wrapping her in a hug.

"I'm not sure if he is yet in the right mood to receive anything from her. But, given time, I'm sure things can be healed."

She didn't completely believe him, but she nodded her head. She tried not to let her glumness show on her face, but she knew she had failed when Charles kissed her nose.

"Why don't I read to you?" he suggested. "What do you have at the moment?" He released her from the hug and grabbed her hand, leading her out of the study and into the sitting room.

"*Descendants of Avalon: Romanaugh's Curse,*" Annabelle replied, settling herself down onto his lap once he was in their favourite armchair. She snuggled into his side and closed her eyes as he began to read.

"In a castle, deep in the woods, shrouded in mist, a young woman fights for family, honour and love."

About the Author

Catherine Price lives just outside of Bath, UK, and has a love of 18th and 19th Century history.

She has two degrees in History and Heritage studies which she uses to give authenticity to her novels.

She is also the creator and host of The Addicted Austenite Podcast, with weekly episodes that cover everything to do with Jane Austen.

Printed in Great Britain
by Amazon